A Kind of Perfect

Christine Schimpf

This is a work of fiction. Names, characters, places, and incidents either are the product of the author's imagination or are used fictitiously, and any resemblance to actual persons living or dead, business establishments, events, or locales, is entirely coincidental.

A Christmas Kind of Perfect
COPYRIGHT 2017 by Christine Schimpf

All rights reserved. No part of this book may be used or reproduced in any manner whatsoever without written permission of the author or Pelican Ventures, LLC except in the case of brief quotations embodied in critical articles or reviews.

eBook editions are licensed for your personal enjoyment only. eBooks may not be re-sold, copied or given to other people. If you would like to share an eBook edition, please purchase an additional copy for each person you share it with.

Contact Information: titleadmin@pelicanbookgroup.com

All scripture quotations, unless otherwise indicated, are taken from the Holy Bible, New International Version(R), NIV(R), Copyright 1973, 1978, 1984, 2011 by Biblica, Inc.™ Used by permission of Zondervan. All rights reserved worldwide. www.zondervan.com

Cover Art by *Nicola Martinez*

Prism is a division of Pelican Ventures, LLC
www.pelicanbookgroup.com PO Box 1738 *Aztec, NM * 87410

The Triangle Prism logo is a trademark of Pelican Ventures, LLC

Publishing History
Prism Edition, 2017
Electronic Edition ISBN 978-1-5223-9775-5
Paperback Edition ISBN 978-1-5223-9777-9
Published in the United States of America

Dedication

To Jasmine,
If you use the gifts God has blessed you with and
believe in your dreams,
they really do come true.
Love you forever, Nana

For I know the plans I have for you, declares the LORD, plans for welfare and not for evil, to give you a future and a hope.

~Jeremiah 29:11

1

Lower Manhattan, New York

Lila almost tripped over her suitcase as she swept into her apartment. Hand to chest, she willed the panic to subside. It seemed that everywhere she went lately, she saw a tall, broad-shouldered man who reminded her of...*him*. Her first love. He was even showing up in her dreams.

Taking a deep breath, she locked the door and kicked off her high-heels. She dragged the suitcase to her bedroom and quickly unpacked as if by doing so she could set memories from ten years ago back in the closet of her mind where they belonged.

It hadn't mattered where her book signing was or that she'd been out on the west coast working on the movie versions of her books, Conrad haunted her.

Ah, the mind of an author was a terrifying place at times. She'd been working too hard. At least that's the excuse she gave herself. Settling into more comfortable clothes she headed to the kitchen.

Lila walked to the window of her apartment cradling a cup of chamomile tea sweetened with honey. She watched the street traffic below, which reminded her of a busy ant colony. How she wished the city would sleep, if only for one night. Oh, the blessed silence. She'd walk for miles. Better yet, she'd run. Although Lila feared the attempt wouldn't be easy. Like so many other activities she used to enjoy doing, she'd abandoned running since moving to the Big Apple years ago.

She padded over to her favorite chair, a chaise longue in dire need of new fabric, and snuggled in like a fat cat finding its spot. The chair stuck out compared to the eclectic-themed room, but Lila refused to reupholster the piece despite the persuasive arguments from her friends. In an odd sort of way, Lila drew comfort from the inanimate object. They shared the same flaw—an inability to fit in with their surroundings.

Lila's bones ached. Now that she was back in the city, her life would return to normal. She'd hibernate for the next few weeks and start outlining her next book. Ugh. At this point, she'd much rather clean her uncle's morning catch of fish.

Goodness, what had made her think of her uncle? He'd died years ago.

Reaching for the remote, she flicked on the receiver. Sounds from an acoustic guitar filled the room. *Ooh, much better*. She placed her emptied cup near her phone on the end table, leaned her head back on the cushion, and stared up at the ceiling.

Her smartphone buzzed. *Ahh*. The phone always seemed to ring at the worst of times, scaring her half to death. The clock had barely moved five minutes, and she'd bet her last chocolate donut that her agent Andrea was calling with another idea for a book tour. Lila swiped the call through. With tired eyes and a worn-out spirit, she forced a pleasant tone. Sounding irritated was not how Lila wanted to present herself. "Hello."

"Hi, I'm calling for Lila Clark."

Lila's heart stopped as if she'd skidded on ice and slammed her vehicle into a fire hydrant. This wasn't Andrea. She recognized the sing-song melody in the caller's voice, so reminiscent of someone from the past. Was her memory going as well as her stamina?

"This is her. Is this—?"

"It's Melanie Lange. Actually, it's Melanie Winters now, from Sister Bay. Remember me?"

Lila bolted upright in her chair, her back ramrod straight, and her melancholy mood chased off by the sound of her best friend's voice. Melanie. "Oh, my gosh. Melanie? Are you kidding? It's been a few years since we've talked, but of course I remember you. How are you?" Photographs flashed in Lila's mind, whisking her out of her apartment and plopping her onto a pier next to the girl she considered more a sister than a friend, their feet dangling in the water, faces tanned with the afternoon sun.

"I'm well." Melanie giggled on the other end as if she were still a young girl.

She sounded exactly the same. Lila's heart warmed, listening to Melanie's pleasant laughter. "I can't tell you how good your voice sounds. It's been too long."

"I'm glad I called even though it took a while for me to muster up the guts."

"Is everything OK?" A stab pricked at Lila's heart as she realized the courage Melanie had to muster for her to call. How things had changed over the years between them.

"Lila, I wasn't certain what to do, so I decided to pick up the phone."

"What's going on?" Lila nibbled on her bottom lip, her interest piqued. She only hoped she could help.

"It's about my store, Window Shopping."

Lila released her breath. "Go on."

"Sales were up until this summer when the village board voted for a May-to-September construction project. The streets were demolished, heavy equipment moved in and along with total devastation as if a tornado passed through here. My store sales plummeted."

"Was your store accessible to customers?"

"Sure, if they were willing to climb over giant boulders or walk through construction zones. To be honest, the tourist season hit an all-time low. Water Front Restaurant and Summer Kitchen closed over the summer. They said it wouldn't pay to remain open."

Lila pressed her shoulder blades against the back of the lounge chair. "Oh, no. Is the rebuilding over now?"

"Yes, but the lack of revenue has left me, well, in the lurch."

"What do you mean?" Lila wasn't an expert in small business operations.

"My accountant was here today. She told me if I don't think of a way to increase sales, I'm looking at closing my doors at the end of the year. I need an influx of revenue and fast. But money isn't the only issue."

Lila scooted off the chaise longue and walked across the room to a solid maple desk. She pulled out the leather padded chair and seated herself, poised to write a check. "There's more?" The poor thing, as if she needed another problem.

"The vultures are circling." Melanie lowered her voice as if sharing a top-secret recipe.

Lila giggled, trying to soften the moment.

"Vultures?" She leaned forward and placed her chin in her free hand.

Melanie sighed. "I've been getting visits from interested investors who want to buy me out. They're assuming I'm in trouble, but I won't sell or even consider it. The store is my life, the reason I get up every morning. It means the world to me, and I refuse to give it away when times get tough."

Melanie loved her store as much as Lila loved writing. Lila's heart ached for Melanie, but what could she do? Melanie was in Sister Bay, and Lila lived in New York. "Oh, Mel, I'm sorry the store is struggling, but how can I help?"

Melanie's tone brightened. "Remember Fall Fest?"

Lila would never forget Sister Bay's last big festival of the season—live music, food booths, a parade... She'd spent the day with him ducking in and out of the quaint shops dotting the water's edge, sharing hot cider, enjoying the festival's music, and those tender, wet kisses in the dark—

"Lila, are you still there?"

Melanie's voice pulled Lila out of her daydream. "Ah...yes. Right here."

"With the construction over and our village brand-spanking new again...Well, I was wondering if you weren't too busy."

What on earth was she getting at? The suspense was killing her. "For crying out loud, Mel, please ask me."

"How about the store hosting a book signing for your latest book during Fall Fest?"

Melanie rattled the request out so fast it took Lila a moment to realize what she said. She sat back in her chair and repeated it in her own head. Wait a minute.

This was not what she'd been expecting. She was anticipating Melanie asking her for a personal loan of some kind. If she went back to Sister Bay, she might run into her ex-boyfriend for real this time and that was something she wasn't prepared for.

"I-I'm not sure I can put a trip together that quickly. Plus, I owe my agent the first fifty pages for my next book."

Melanie sighed. "Oh, you're working on another book already?"

"Not really, but I should be. I literally walked in the door from a grueling East Coast book tour as well as at trip to California for a movie deal. To tell you the truth, I'm a little burned out right now."

"Well, I bet I know what you need." Melanie's tone was as matter-of-fact as the commentator on the six o'clock news.

Lila exhaled a slow, easy breath, allowed her shoulders to fall forward, and tucked a strand of hair behind her ear. She couldn't remember the last time she'd walked barefoot along the water's edge even though she believed it was the very practice that filled her spirit and fueled her purpose. She'd allowed that connection to break, to fall by the wayside like an old hobby she no longer enjoyed. Was that why she was struggling with an idea for her next book? Lila's slipped her bottom lip between her teeth. "OK, Mel, I'm listening."

"A little home sweet home. You could arrive a bit early, and we'll catch up at the store. It'll be like old times. Oh, Lila, please say yes."

"Oh, Mel, that sounds wonderful. I could use some serious time off. But I'm not sure I can manage it."

"Are you kidding me? Your agent works for you, doesn't she?"

True. "She does."

"Promise her those fifty pages will be in her hand on your return."

"She may agree with that idea. It's been forever since I've taken some time off. In fact, I can't remember my last vacation."

"If it was when you had to cancel your trip for my wedding because of your appendicitis attack, you are long overdue for a visit."

"That was four years ago! Poor Aunt Cathy had to fly out and take care of me for weeks, bless her heart. Maybe you're right, it's time."

"That sounds like a yes to me. Am I right?"

Lila paused. She didn't consider herself impulsive, but she craved more spontaneity in her life. Over the years, she'd grown to be so rigid in her routine. She drew in a deep breath, garnering courage.

"I'll do it. I'm meeting with my agent tomorrow night, and I'll figure something out to make this happen. It's time for a visit and I'd love the opportunity to help you out, Mel."

"I'm so glad I mustered up the nerve to call you. I can't wait for you to arrive."

"Me, too. We'll talk soon, I promise. I'll text you the details."

"And I'll get started on some of the marketing. The whole county is going to go wild once they find out you're coming. Look out Sister Bay. Lila Clark is on her way."

"My ears hear a chant from our cheerleading days." Lila giggled.

"I've still got it," Melanie sang back. "Travel safe."

"I will and Mel?"

"Yeah?"

"Thanks for calling. I needed this."

"I love you, dear friend."

"Me, too."

After the call, Lila paced across her living room floor. Talking with Mel again felt like eating funnel cake at a summer fair. Going home sounded better and better to recharge. She was sure the chances of running into her ex-boyfriend were slim, and the idea of him attending her book signing was out of the question. She picked up the phone and dialed the only other person in Sister Bay, Wisconsin, who would care about her pending arrival. "I'm coming home," she said before her Aunt Cathy could even say a greeting.

2

Bong. The grandfather clock, one of the eccentric pieces Lila had inherited from her parents stood in the corner of her great room, chiming the quarter hour. Was the antique trying to tell her to pitch Melanie's idea to Andrea? Lila's agent stood at the kitchen island looking at the appetizers Lila had prepared for their meeting.

What approach would be best to break the ice? She could suggest the book signing Melanie wanted her to do, a vacation, or both. After all, her last trip home was close to five years ago. She expected Andrea would want her to get busy on her next book. She steeled herself for an uncomfortable conversation and hoped she could reach the friend and not the agent.

Lila curled her feet under her in the club chair. "A good friend of mine called last night."

Andrea turned away from the island, a small plate of appetizers in hand. "Really? Who?"

"Melanie Winters. She owns Window Shopping, a gift shop and bookstore in Sister Bay up in Door County, Wisconsin. She asked if I would come home and do a book signing for my latest book at her store."

Andrea stilled. "Oh? When does she want you to do that? You just returned home."

Andrea was right but going home to recharge offered more appeal. "During Sister Bay's Fall Fest."

"Fall Fest? Sounds like something I'd enjoy."

Lila leaned forward in her chair. "It's the last big

festival for the year and usually draws hundreds of tourists." She awaited Andrea's response.

"And who's Melanie?"

"A friend who is more like a sister to me."

"Why does she want you?" Andrea left her plate on the island and turned around to face Lila.

Maybe this wouldn't be as difficult as Lila imagined—so far, so good, but her comment caused Lila to ponder if Andrea ever had a friend like Melanie.

Lila shrugged. "Why not? I'm a local author, successful, and although we don't get together as much as we'd like, we used to be good friends. It'll also help the store's bottom line, which, according to Melanie, needs a boost."

"Isn't Door County a big tourist area for Wisconsin? What happened to her store sales?"

"Heavy road construction this summer. The project killed tourism. Many of the other local shops are in the same situation. Some of them decided not to open for the summer."

Andrea wrinkled her nose as if an unpleasant odor entered the room. "What happens if you don't do the signing?"

Lila hoped she wasn't losing Andrea's empathy. "She's looking at closing her doors at the end of the year." Lila allowed her statement to resonate and hoped it would touch the compassionate side of Andrea. "To be honest, I could use some time off."

Andrea frowned. She walked across the kitchen to one of the massive windows in the great room. Her crocodile heels clicked on the travertine floor like the typewriter keys of years gone by. She wore her jet-black hair in a chic bob accentuating her violet eyes. The expensive New York brand name tweed pencil skirt and ivory silk blouse clung to her thin frame. Oversized pearls hung at her neck, concealing sharp-edged collarbones. "You're not thinking of actually going through with this, are you?"

Lila twirled a strand of hair around her finger. "I am."

"We talked about another series I could pitch to Jim over at Stonewood Publishers, remember? Besides I'm doing my best to secure the best publishing deal I can for you. It's my job to keep the business side of things running smoothly. I'm sorry, Lila, but you don't have the wiggle room to take time off. I wish I could say otherwise, but I can't."

Lila shrugged. She'd grown accustomed to the drill. "I understand, but I'm low on inspiration at the moment. I think getting out of New York for a while would do me good. Don't you?"

Was that the problem? The well of creative ideas had gone dry? Lila stared into a corner of the room, nibbling on her bottom lip, a habit she thought she broke years ago. She'd been reckless with everything that grounded her in life. She'd nearly abandoned her faith, and going home never occurred to her. But there was a good reason for that decision until now, and his name was Conrad Hamilton. Living with her shame in Manhattan was hard enough, returning to Sister Bay might dredge up the past, but she'd deal with that later. Melanie needed her, and Lila wasn't going to let her down.

Andrea turned away from the window. "I understand why you want out of the city. I hate to make an issue over this, but we're both aware of the situation over at Stonewood. The pressure is on, and Jim's getting tired of the grind. I'm afraid we might lose him. The next editor may not be as eager to work with us."

Lila exhaled. "I'd love to do this. This last book tour drained me. Don't you ever desire to get out of New York—to recharge if nothing else?"

"Why would I want to get out of New York?" Andrea laughed through her words. "It's one of the most exciting cities in the world. There's nowhere else on earth like New York or anywhere I'd rather be."

"True for you, my friend, but sometimes the city closes in on me. This is one of those times."

Andrea walked toward Lila. She kicked off her heels and slid into the companion chair. "You shouldn't be unhappy. You're thirty-two years old with a stellar career as a best-selling novelist and with the movie rights you'll continue on that path. You need to keep your momentum if you want to maintain this lifestyle. You live in this beautifully decorated penthouse apartment in Manhattan, shop on Fifth Avenue, and can vacation wherever you please. I'd kill to be in your shoes."

As Andrea's largest client, this wasn't good news. But Lila was listening to her heart for the first time in years. "I need a break, and I'll be helping out an old friend."

The last glimmer of sunlight faded away, allowing a bleak darkness to creep into the room. Along with it, came an uninvited chill, sending a shiver up Lila's spine. She picked up a remote and with a click of a button, the keystone fireplace whooshed into motion. Bright orange flames danced on blackened logs.

Lila closed her eyes and remembered the autumn season in full swing in Door County: the scent of outdoor fires, the showcase of color, and the bite in the air at dusk. How she'd missed the fall extravaganza that walked into the village like a welcomed guest.

Andrea laced her fingers in front of her. For a moment, she looked like a stern elementary school principal. "I don't understand. What could be more important to you than securing your next contract?"

Silence found a spot between them and settled in. The grandfather clock chimed, reminding Lila time was moving right along.

"OK," Andrea drawled, "how long will you be gone?" She lifted a glass of cucumber infused water to her lips. The sound of resignation in her voice as clear as the antioxidant beverage she held in her hand.

"A couple of months. After the book signing at Window Shopping, I'll recharge my batteries and hit the ground writing."

"So, you'd be back here Christmas week? I want to remind you, Stonewood wants new contracts signed by New Year's Eve."

Lila reclined in her chair. "I'll hand you the fifty pages on my return. That should satisfy everyone."

"You realize you're going to miss out on Stonewood's Halloween costume ball. You remember how much fun it was last year? You might meet someone this year."

The thought of staying for the ball almost made Lila laugh. Every year, Stonewood Publishers threw a fantastic Halloween party. Writers, editors, the press, and fans with deep pockets arrived dressed in elaborate costumes for the event. She winced as she remembered last year's bash. Although she'd met someone at the event, in the end, the spark died and the relationship soon followed suit. It shouldn't surprise her anymore. It was so much like all of her other relationships over the years—dismal failures. But after the hurt she inflicted on her ex-boyfriend, she didn't deserve to find love again. Sometimes second chances never came.

"I bet your lease on this apartment, you'll be back well before Christmas. You're going to miss it. The city is addictive." Andrea flashed a genuine smile in Lila's direction.

Lila breathed a sigh of relief with Andrea's change of heart. She didn't want to upset her or Jim and risk losing everything she worked for over the last ten years. Andrea wasn't wrong. Lila was sure to miss New York, but at the same time, something was pulling her toward this trip.

Andrea lifted her glass. "When do you leave?"

"Fall Fest is next weekend. I booked the 7:00 AM flight into Green Bay International." This was really happening. A fresh surge of excitement pulsed through her veins. She hadn't felt this way since her first book launch.

Andrea smirked. "Tomorrow morning?"

Lila took a deep breath. "Yes."

"Wow. This reminds me of something my mother used to say, 'No rest for the weary.'"

Lila giggled. "I guess not."

"What about phone service? I want to stay in touch."

"I should receive good enough coverage, but it might be spotty at times."

Andrea raised her glass in Lila's direction as if holding a glass of champagne. "Here's to a great trip to Door County and back home again."

Lila smiled and returned the toast. "Thanks for understanding. It makes it easier for me to leave."

Andrea's smile faded, replaced with a frown. "You make it sound like you're never coming back."

"Don't be silly. Of course, I'm coming home." Lila flashed a reassuring smile. "The last thing I want to happen is to lose a bet."

Andrea chuckled. "I believe that." She returned her plate to the table. "I should scoot. I'm meeting Jim for dinner tonight. I'll be sure to fill him in on your news." She grabbed her expensive blue bag and headed for the door.

Lila hugged her friend good-bye, and Andrea blew Lila a kiss as she made her way down the hall to the elevators.

Lila leaned her head against the cold metal door. What was she doing standing there? She needed to pack.

3

Lila slipped behind the wheel of the sport utility vehicle she'd rented at Green Bay International. Despite the early departure, LaGuardia Airport churned out a healthy dose of chaos. Would she ever adjust to the warp speed of life in New York? In years gone by, she'd always preferred the smaller terminals, the scenic route to a destination, or the mom-and-pop restaurants. How she ended up in Lower Manhattan still surprised her.

Music filled the cab, and with a surge of adrenaline, Lila merged onto Highway 57, heading straight for Sturgeon Bay. She was filled with childlike ache to squiggle her toes in the dirt, to lie in the grass, and to roll side-over-side in the leaves. Although a nip chilled the air, she cracked the window and enjoyed the crisp pine scent. She shivered, and as silly as it was, she flipped on the heat to toast her feet as she drove home. Color surrounded her on both sides of the road like exploding fireworks on the Fourth of July—scarlet reds, blackened browns, leprechaun greens, gingered yellows.

Her heart picked up its pace as the magic of autumn hit her full force. Memories came next, drowning out the lyrics playing in the background. Her mind wandered to celebrations around a bonfire, her mother's smile, the crunch of leaves under her feet and canning applesauce with her Aunt Cathy. She recalled the scolding she and Melanie received for not peeling the entire apple before dropping the slices into the bubbling water, and she laughed. "You've got to do a better job, ladies, or the skins will end up in our sauce."

Lila lifted her shoulders and stretched her neck, a practice she'd mastered to relieve tension. She inhaled a slow, deep cleansing breath. She was on sabbatical. "Let all your worries go." Her yoga instructor's words whispered in her ear as if he was sitting right beside her. She wouldn't consider herself a fan of exercise, but it acted as a good replacement for the morning runs she no longer enjoyed. As the miles passed, she reminisced the carefree days of her youth.

Lila had met Melanie in the back row of their elementary school class. As the years passed, they kept each other's secrets, and Lila believed nothing could break a friendship as strong as theirs. The sisterhood-like ties bonded them together, making Lila believe they would share the relationship throughout their lives.

When the college years arrived, Lila chose a different path, pursuing journalism in Chicago while Melanie chased after a business degree at the University of Milwaukee. The occasional visit home for the holidays and the lure of new relationships worked against them. The move to New York had severed their bond in a way that felt like forever.

Lila crossed over the bridge and began the ten-mile stretch through Sturgeon Bay. She pulled over to the curb and shot a few pictures of the apple-red barns with their brand-new tin roofs. Not long after, she picked up Highway 42 toward Egg Harbor and Fish Creek. The cherry orchards and harvested cornfields peppered the landscape. Her mouth watered remembering her mother's homemade cherry pie. Nothing in New York would ever compare to the homegrown cherries she took for granted as a child.

The Cupola House in Egg Harbor was now on her right. The rocky shoreline on her left reappeared. She curled along the highway moving with traffic through Fish Creek. If only she had time to stop at Shipwrecked Pub for a spicy bowl of their renowned chili. She searched her purse for one of her power granola bars. Sighing, she found one and devoured it before the next curve in the road.

She scanned the countryside for the red-planked Anderson Barn in Ephraim, which would mean Sister Bay was close. Lila slowed as the road wound around towering birch trees, stout evergreens, and underbrush showcasing paprika-colored leaves. Bethany Lutheran Church's steeple rose to the north as if guiding her path. The brilliant colors surrounded her like a thick warm quilt, and the door to her past she'd thought she closed began creaking open.

Lifting her foot off the gas, Lila followed the tree-lined streets along the water's edge and coasted into Sister Bay. The newly paved roads welcomed her into the small and only incorporated village in Door County. Kitty-corner from the marina, the familiar Al Johnson's Swedish Restaurant acted as an anchor for the retail shop district and for new businesses such as Drink Coffee and Cookie Lady. Too bad the goats weren't on the grass-covered roof at Al's, but their season ended every year at this time.

Lila scolded herself. Now was not the time for sightseeing. She needed to find a parking space. She drove down Bay Shore Drive, made a U-turn, and traveled back through again and found a spot right across the street from Window Shopping.

Lila stepped into the street among the swirling leaves picked up and spun almost magically by a passing wind. She never thought of herself as nostalgic, but the giddiness of a child filled her as she checked for oncoming cars making her way across the street to Window Shopping. Now she was home and about to see her best friend.

Lila swung open the wooden gate leading to the store, causing a creak that reminded her of the sound her grandmother's rocking chair. She walked up the gray-toned stone walkway, keeping a careful eye on her steps. Why on earth had she worn heels today? An expansive yellow-and-white-striped awning that protected an enormous display window caught her attention. Behind the glass, a lazy array of pumpkins, gourds, and baskets of apples was scattered across the floor. It was as if she had walked into the October page of a Norman Rockwell calendar. Lila's fingers drifted along the tops of scarlet mums the soft petals caressing her fingers. Melanie put a lot of work into this yard.

Lila pulled open a screened door. An oversized wreath showcasing dried lavender, roses, and mums, the same flowers in the front yard, hung in the middle of a pane of frosted glass. The words *Window Shopping* were etched in a semicircle above. She wrapped her fingers around the brass lever, positioned her shoulder square on the doorframe and pushed. A tinkling bell greeted her along with the strong scent of gingerbread, taking her back to her mother's kitchen.

She gravitated toward the voices coming from the other side of the room, passing by a pair of club chairs and a matching ottoman. She grazed her fingers over a fisherman's knot afghan draped over the chair. She wished she were wrapped inside its warmth with a good book.

Melanie stood behind an oversized antique counter. Her Italian dark curls were piled high on her head, secured in place with rhinestone pins reminiscent of those she'd loved in years past. Her cheeks were flushed as she handed over the striped paper bag bearing the store's logo to a customer. Lila slowed her step. Melanie appeared healthier and happier in all the years she could remember. Lila's heart melted when her friend noticed her.

"Lila! You're here." Melanie stepped around the counter and walked toward her. She opened her arms wide. "So, this is what a famous author looks like."

Lila gasped. "Oh, my word. You're..."

Melanie grinned, taking Lila back years to their mischievous era, and patted her tummy with small hands. "Pregnant? Yes. I've got twins in here."

"Oh, Mel, congratulations." Lila couldn't be happier for her friend. Melanie always wanted a large family. She wrapped her arms around her best friend with care. Although tiny lines etched the familiar eyes of the woman who used to be the closest person to her, Lila still saw the friend she'd met in grade school. An overwhelming sense of peace prevailed. She was home, and for the first time in years, Lila wanted it all back.

"It's so good to see you, Mel. I've missed you. And twins? How is that possible? You look fantastic." Lila brought her hands to her face, flabbergasted with Melanie's unexpected news.

Melanie lifted her small shoulders. "Jack Winters knew full well that twins were a possibility with me, but he married me anyway. We expect Benjamin and

Brian before Christmas."

Lila shook her head, her eyes wide. "You haven't lost your sense of humor. How is Jack?"

"He's busy running all over the county, but the engineer in him is happy." Melanie guided Lila's steps behind the checkout counter.

Rolls of wrapping paper, ribbon, striped gift bags, and tissue cluttered the area. "Sounds like he's doing a lot of traveling."

"He is, but he's transferring to a desk job in the Sturgeon Bay office the first of the year." Using a soft bristled brush, Melanie swept the remnants of ribbon and paper into a small garbage pail.

"I'm glad, especially now with the babies coming." Lila gestured toward Melanie's bulging tummy.

Melanie rested her hands on her back. "Believe me, so am I."

"Are you sure you need my help? The store gives a divine impression both inside and out. In order to enjoy anything close to what's in your front yard, I have to get myself down to Central Park. And although it's beautiful, it's not this."

"Really? How far is it from where you live?" Melanie leaned against the counter.

"It's not far, but with all the foot traffic, it takes too long to get there, and by the time I do, it's lost its appeal." In fact, Lila didn't want to tell her how long it was since she'd been there.

Melanie raised an eyebrow. "That sounds awful. I choose not to live without the birds in the morning or the grass beneath my feet. Even the winter months provide a solace that mends the soul." Melanie's eyes held a hint of concern. "You used to love those things too, Lila."

"I still do, but living in the big city is a different way of life. Honestly, Mel, how did you create such a beautiful front entrance to the store? It's so welcoming."

"Before Jack's father sold the property to us, we did a complete renovation. He even hired professional landscapers to give the place 'my style,' as he called it. He understood how much I loved the outdoors, so he filled the front lawn with flowering bushes."

Lila laid a hand on her chest. "That's amazing."

Melanie gestured toward the coffee bar. "I considered it a very generous thing for him to do. God bless him. The only project left is something I call the ski chalet. It's a small addition with benches and a gas fireplace at the back of the store."

"A ski chalet? Why?" Lila followed Melanie toward the bar, absorbing the intoxicating colors, textures, and scents swirling around her.

"The village board approved a ginormous ski and sled hill at the edge of town. Not too long ago, we all enjoyed an official groundbreaking ceremony. The whole village showed up. It should be finished in time for Christmas. Since there's no lodge being built, in the future, I'd like to attract the business to the store and offer hot cocoa, scones, and I'm considering light sandwiches."

Lila lifted a hand to her forehead. "I envy you and everything going on." Melanie was living the dream Lila gave away. How her life would be different if she'd come home after the internship in Chicago or turned down the job in New York. Her mind wandered. Would she and her first love be married by now, expecting their first baby?

Melanie interrupted Lila's thoughts. "To answer

your question, yes, I need you. Your book signing is a blessing." She gestured Lila toward a quilted-topped stool.

"Still enjoy a chai latte?" Melanie rubbed her palms together.

Lila grinned. "You read my mind. May I help?"

Melanie waved her hand and patted her round belly. "No, no. If I stop moving I tend to cramp up. The boys are beginning to fight for the little space left, and the pain shoots right down my legs. I'll be back in two seconds."

Lila removed her leather jacket and placed it on top of her bag on a neighboring stool. She took a seat and worked off her high heels. They fell on the floor with a muted thud. She massaged her foot working out the kink in the ball of her foot.

The soft strumming of an acoustic guitar and chirping birds filled the space. The rhythm of the chords began to work its magic. Lila's shoulders eased. She scanned the room. Her gaze caught the sparkling stones in a selection of handbags. Crayola-colored umbrellas stood at attention in a metal stand, and earthy brown mittens with burgundy buttons sat on a nearby antique table. The store was loaded with fabrics that wanted to be touched and colors that soothed one's soul. Everything Melanie loved, from almond bread recipes to inspirational plaques to books and so much more.

Lila's breath caught. She brought her fingers to her lips. A solid maple bookcase centered in the room displayed her work. A picture of her taken years ago smiled back at her. Framed newspaper articles stood behind all ten of Lila's books. Melanie created an impressive layout, but, more importantly, it was an endearment that touched her heart.

Melanie turned the corner from the back kitchen holding a tray with two mugs and a plate of scones. She set the tray on the counter and placed the ceramic mugs filled with hot tea down on bamboo coasters. A small basket of cellophane-wrapped chocolates sat between them, each one tied in autumn-colored ribbons.

"So, what do you think of the store?" She placed Lila's mug in front of her, eased onto a stool, and picked up her own.

"I don't want to leave. Do you find that a problem with your people who come in here?" Lila blew the steam that rose from her mug and took her first sip. Hmm, delicious.

"Much of the time, yes." Melanie curled her fingers around her mug. "But when that happens, customers end up spending more money, so it's all good. The big book retailers began to offer small cafés and comfortable spaces with good reason. I try to follow their lead as much as possible, but it's all about overhead for me. I found out the longer a customer stays, the more they buy. First a latte, perhaps a scone, and before long, they're reconsidering the plaque they were admiring earlier."

Lila's brow furrowed. "How do you manage to keep costs low?"

"For one thing, I do as much as I can by myself. I've perfected a recipe for a pretty little cranberry scone, and the lattes are easy with my new coffeemaker. On a rare occasion, I order something special from Al Johnson's. The business owners help each other out when we can, and we never steal each other's bestsellers. Understand?"

Lila frowned. "Not really."

"Do you see the little shop across the street called Drink Coffee and Cookie Lady?"

"I did notice it when I drove into the village."

"They sell some of the best cookies on the peninsula, so that's an item I don't offer here at Window Shopping. Instead, I bake scones." Melanie offered up both hands.

Lila sipped her tea. "Of course, it's like a silent code among you."

"Right," Melanie nodded, "we help support one another and when we need to, we band together. For instance, speaking to the village about snow removal during the winter. That's a hot button because if our customers can't park on the streets, they can't get into our stores."

"So, you're open over the winter?"

Melanie flashed a grin. "I hang on, and we do OK."

Lila eased back into her chair. "I'm beginning to understand that running a store is a lot more than what I'd imagined."

"After Jack, it's one of the loves of my life. Some days are quiet, and that's when I change things around a bit or give the coffeemaker a good vinegar scrub."

Lila laughed along with Melanie. The years that passed between them slipping away. She was back in the company of her best friend. Although there was a sense of camaraderie with friends in New York, those relationships didn't run as deep as the one she once had with Melanie. Lila prayed she could mend what she'd broken between herself and the woman sitting across from her.

Melanie bit into her scone. "The store keeps me

hopping, and you remember how much I love staying busy along with eating scones."

"Oh, yes." Lila giggled and picked up one for herself.

A movement from the back of the room caught her attention. She turned her head—a workman, perhaps—who'd entered the store through the back entrance. His ruffled dark hair and broad shoulders were so familiar. Could it be…?

Melanie cleared her throat. "I'm sorry. I meant to explain but didn't get the chance."

Lila swiveled in her seat to face Melanie. "Explain—"

"Conrad is here. He's finishing up the exit ramp and new door for the disabled. He's such a sweetheart to still do these little projects for me despite how busy he is with Hamilton Construction."

Lila gasped. Conrad, her first and only love, was the last person she wanted to run into in her first few minutes in town. "Are you kidding me?" She caught the panic in her voice and lowered her tone, "Conrad's here?"

"I didn't think it'd be a problem. I mean, it's all good between you two, right? It's been such a long time. I assumed everything—"

"I…" Lila's tongue twisted up in her mouth. She couldn't form a word.

Melanie turned her attention toward Conrad.

Oh, no. Lila reached out to stop her, but it was too late.

"Conrad, come and say hello to Lila," Melanie's clear voice sang to the back of the room.

Lila nibbled on her lower lip.

The one person she hoped to avoid on this trip

walked toward them. Conrad Hamilton. She noticed his dark brooding eyes from across the room. They caught hers and held on, like so many years ago. Lila's breath quickened, and her heartbeat thudded in her ears. With broad shoulders, strong hands, and a no-nonsense stride, he moved in her direction.

Conrad had grown up.

4

Conrad groaned. If he didn't want to run into Lila, he should've thought twice about accepting Melanie's job. Only he was to blame for the situation he was in right now. Melanie told him Lila was coming to town to help out the store, and the local grapevine was buzzing. They were all talking about it at Drink Coffee this morning. Last night, a poster announcing the book signing had stared him straight in the face. He noticed it in the window of Merchant's Meats and Sausage while driving home from Sturgeon Bay.

Conrad's gut signaled him to turn down the job, but he had a soft spot for people like Melanie—good people who worked hard like he did. His business started with the little jobs from the locals, and he vowed never to forget the customers who helped him along the way. Melanie was one of those people.

He brushed away the collected wood shavings from the front of his blue denim shirt and regretted not shaving this morning. Had it been five years since he'd last laid eyes on Lila? Who was he kidding? He remembered exactly how much time passed since he'd seen her. She didn't appear older—thinner maybe, but not older.

Her thick hair was twisted up behind her head, loose strands framing her face. Almond-shaped eyes, the color of milk chocolate, with the power to draw him to her still. He used to lose himself in those eyes. Long, dangling earrings brushed her cheeks as she moved. He smiled when he noticed a pair of heels on the floor underneath her chair. She never did like them.

As he drew close, the scent of lily of the valley filled the space between them. Memories of lazy summer afternoons spent on a blanket with her at Marina Park flooded in: the roar of the waves outside matching his tempo for her on the inside. His jaw tightened. He didn't consider himself a man who kept count of his regrets, but he rued plenty where this woman was concerned.

He shifted his weight, fighting the tight knot forming in his stomach. What could he say to show he'd gotten over her and moved on? "Hello, Lila." The words slipped off his tongue before a second thought. Her name sounded sweet on his lips.

Her natural smile flashed on cue. "Conrad, it's great to see you."

It surprised him how wonderful it was to see her again, in spite of how their relationship ended. "You look well." The curve of her lips took him back to the days of their early dating when he couldn't wait to pick her up, pull her close, and to touch her skin, as smooth and silky as the ice cream sold down at Wilson's.

Melanie shifted in her seat. Was it possible she sensed the undercurrent between him and Lila? "I've been explaining to Lila that you're always here when I need you. Installing the ramp and new door right before the signing was important to me."

Conrad fixed his gaze on Melanie and fought the urge to stare at the woman he failed to go after. "You're welcome. By the way, how's everything going these days?"

Melanie placed a pair of petite hands on her hips.

"Fat and sassy and don't you change the subject."

Lila tossed her head back and laughed. It rang in Conrad's ears, sounding as good as one of his favorite rock songs.

Melanie wore an insistent expression. "Come and join us. I was thinking about how nice it would be to include a riser for the book signing so Lila'd be visible to everyone."

Conrad wished he'd never walked over. Now he was in a difficult situation. He'd rather be swinging a hammer instead of sliding into a seat next to Lila. He tilted his head toward the project waiting for him. "I really should get back at it. My schedule's pretty tight today."

"Oh, I promise it won't take long. Can I get you a coffee or scone?" Melanie inched up her eyebrows.

Conrad raised his hand. "Thank you, no. I've got my thermos in the back, and I ate breakfast." He took a seat on a stool next to Lila and lifted a foot to rest on the lower rung. "So, when do you need this riser installed, and where do you want it?" As far as he could remember, Lila wasn't much for the limelight. Of course, that was years ago in a different time and place.

"Is tomorrow too soon? I realize its late notice. Tell me if you can't manage it," Melanie begged a favor.

Lila pressed her shoulders back into her chair and slipped one leg over the other with ease. Pink-painted toes winked up at him. He used to tickle those toes until she begged him to stop. He cleared his throat. Where was his head going? He fished around for his smartphone. When he found it, he swiped his oversized fingers across the screen. This was for Melanie.

After checking his digital calendar, Conrad

slipped his phone back into his shirt pocket and gave Melanie a smile. "Well, I don't want to disappoint a regular customer. The earliest I can schedule it is tomorrow night after you close. It shouldn't take me too long."

"Perfect. Conrad, you're a lifesaver. If you could place it up front, that would be ideal. That way, the overflow customers will get a glimpse of Lila through the big display window." Melanie clapped.

"You got it. I'll pick up the lumber from your storage unit tonight." Conrad faced Lila. "Would you like a set of stairs? They fit in the center of the riser allowing you to walk down and join the audience at any time."

Lila gave him an appreciative smile.

Conrad stood. Unable to fight the urge, he shifted his gaze from Melanie to Lila.

Her face softened. Her lips barely turning up at the edges. Conrad recognized the gesture but wasn't prepared for the impact of how much he missed it. It took every ounce of stamina not to smile. Instead, he managed a perfunctory nod and headed to the back of the room.

5

Lila brought her mug of chai to her lips and took a few sips. The delicious frothy cinnamon brew warmed her insides. Why was it that most men seemed to improve with age?

Obviously, Conrad's work suited him—his body strong and muscular. His thick, rounded shoulders caused the fabric in his denim shirt to strain. Chiseled cheeks and a forgotten morning shave made it impossible not to notice his attractiveness. He had matured into a man who possessed magnetism most women, including her, would find hard to ignore.

Lila closed her eyes, imagining being wrapped in those big bear arms again. When she'd been in his arms, nothing else in the world mattered. She worked a strand of her hair around her finger, over and over and over.

Melanie nudged Lila's arm. "Lila?"

Lila jerked her hand away from her hair. *Oh, great. What did I miss?*

Melanie tilted her head. "You were a million miles away. Do you remember what happened when Mrs. White caught you daydreaming? You wrote a hundred times on the chalkboard 'I will not daydream.'"

Lila shifted her gaze from Melanie to catch a glance at Conrad's retreating form. Was he grinning? "That's not true."

"It happened all the time. I'll bet that's the catalyst to your success in writing. Now your make-believe world has come to life."

Lila adjusted her blouse on her shoulders. "I guess you're right. But really, what did you ask me?"

"Did you like Conrad's suggestion?"

"Oh, about installing the set of stairs?"

Melanie grinned as if she suspected Lila's thoughts. "Yes."

"It's a good idea." Was it possible Conrad remembered her distaste for attention?

Melanie squiggled up her petite nose. "I hope that wasn't too uncomfortable for you."

Lila feigned nonchalance. She placed her emptied cup on the bamboo coaster and rubbed her forehead. "You mean with Conrad?"

"Was it a little déjà vu-ey?" Melanie's eyes twinkled.

Lila wasn't sure she was ready to open up about Conrad. She'd locked away all of her hurt and disappointment when their relationship ended, but she ached for the closeness she and Melanie once shared. The years that passed were like a chasm between them. When their eyes met, Lila decided it was time to close the gap. "It was, a bit."

"Conrad hasn't changed. He's still the same sweet, big-hearted lug he's always been."

Lila held back her laughter. "Lug? That's the last word I'd use to describe a man like Conrad."

Melanie waved a hand. "He's like a big brother to me. May I tell you something else? I don't think Suzanne Matthews deserves him. Despite her attractiveness or success in real estate."

Lila's heart dropped to her stomach, as if she'd read her first rejection letter. She busied her hands rearranging the wrapped chocolates in the basket.

"Conrad's dating Suzanne?" Asking the question was as hard for Lila as believing it could be true. Of course, she didn't expect him to be single all these years, did she?

Melanie brushed a hand across Lila's shoulders. "I'm sorry. I assumed someone told you. They've been together for a couple of years now. The rumor mill has it she expects a ring this Christmas." Melanie's eyes softened. "It took him a long time to get over you. He began playing volleyball in the summers and joined Jack's bowling league in the winter. You remember how he hated bowling, right? He was never home. He ate out a lot. Started hanging out at the Bier Zot, and, well, you can imagine what went along with that—too many bad decisions with all the wrong people."

Lila stared at the wood-planked floor, devouring the information. "How did his relationship with Suzanne start?"

"Jack mentioned she started working part-time at the bowling alley shortly after Conrad joined the team. She's a hard woman not to notice, if you get my meaning, and one foot does follow the other."

Who could forget Suzanne with her inherited Norwegian bone structure and the rare shade of captivating green eyes? "From what I remember, she'd always been attracted to him."

"And that may be enough."

Lila scowled. "Is that what's going to make a good marriage?"

"People get married for all kinds of reasons. Trust me, Lila. In a village this size, I listen when people talk and hear plenty, especially running the store."

"I suppose Suzanne is still as gorgeous as always?"

Melanie smoothed her hands down her sides, protruding her round belly.

Lila rolled her eyes. Melanie's sense of humor was as strong as ever.

"You remember she studied ballet, so she has that svelte body." She drawled out the words in an attempt at a French accent.

Lila appreciated the comic relief. The conversation had turned more serious and she didn't want that.

Melanie bent toward Lila and lowered her voice. "I need to flat out ask you something."

"Do you have any other style?" Lila smirked. Their old relationship was beginning a new chapter between them.

"How did it end between you? Conrad wouldn't talk about it to anyone. He and Jack were tight for a while, before Suzanne entered the picture."

Lila exhaled a long, tired breath. "The internship in Chicago left me with little time to make it home. The job was demanding, a lot more was expected of me than I had anticipated, and I was exhausted. I told myself it was only for a few months. But, somehow, I grew to enjoy the pressure. It pushed my writing to the next level. When it ended and the opportunity to connect with an agent in New York came up, I grabbed it. The book deals kept coming, and then the movie rights—it snowballed from there. In the end, Conrad didn't want to leave Sister Bay, and I couldn't turn the job down. We broke up over the phone. Can you imagine?"

"Oh, Lila, was it worth it? I mean, everyone thought you two…" Melanie lifted her shoulders as if to indicate they would get married.

Lila moved her mug in circles over the counter.

"My career is terrific. Everything I ever wanted in that department came true."

Melanie laced her fingers and rested her hands on her belly like a shelf. "I hear a *but* between those words. Is something missing?"

This was the part of their friendship that Lila missed the most—her friend's ability to read her without judgment. "It's wonderful in New York but lonely at the same time."

Melanie's drooped shoulders brought Lila the realization that something about New York troubled Melanie.

"How long does it take you to write a book?"

Lila drew in a deep breath. "About nine months. After it's launched, we tour for the next three."

"Let me get this straight. You released a new book, finished a three-month book tour, and now you're expected to start all over again?"

Lila nodded. "That sounds about right. That's the job, and I get paid well to do it."

Melanie moaned. "Are you kidding me? That sounds like a lot of pressure to finish the book and more to promote it. All I do here is have fun interacting with people. Sure, I need to keep the books and make enough money to stay afloat but that's about it."

Lila shrugged and smiled. "It can be troublesome until you implement a structure to organize your thoughts and ideas. It took me a while, but I've got a system that works now."

"What about love? How does that fit into a writer's life?"

Lila hoped Melanie's perception didn't penetrate the false bravado she was portraying. She shrugged. "I've dated, but nothing ever panned out. My schedule's a little too chaotic—maybe one day."

"I don't like the sound of that. There's always time for love. Jack and I experience great times that we realize we'll never forget and bad moments when we go head-to-head, but I wouldn't give up our marriage for anything. We understand each other the way you and Conrad used to."

Lila shifted her gaze from Melanie to where Conrad disappeared. What was he doing? She fought the urge to go investigate.

"I'm sorry. I shouldn't keep bringing up your relationship with Conrad," Melanie apologized drawing Lila back to their conversation.

Lila waved her hand as if shooing away a pesky fly in the room. "It's OK. You've always been smarter and luckier in life in so many ways. I wish I possessed some of your good sense."

Melanie walked around the counter and took a seat next to Lila. She laid her hand on Lila's knee. "It's no accident or coincidence that you're here, Lila. And luck? I don't believe in it. For whatever reason, you're right where you should be. Your decision to come home is exactly what you need, a breath of homespun air. You can reset your priorities in life."

Lila nodded, giving serious thought to what Melanie told her.

"How long can you stay?"

Lila laced her fingers together. "About two months."

"Two months." Melanie gasped. "That puts you back in New York right before Christmas."

"I sold your idea to my agent last night. She wasn't thrilled about the visit, but she's agreed. I promised her the first couple of chapters of my next book. It shouldn't be a problem—I hope."

"Good. What are you going to write about next?" Melanie asked.

Lila lifted her eyebrows. "No idea. I'm hoping to be inspired while I'm here."

"Are you open to a new adventure?" Melanie widened her eyes.

Spontaneity always was an attribute Lila wanted. "Sure."

"Any chance you'd be interested in a part-time job?"

"Me? Why?"

Melanie sighed. "I semi-promised Jack I'd close the store early beginning in November. He's noticed how tired I've become these last couple of weeks. But I really hate to do that, especially with the holidays approaching. After the summer tourism season, it's the second-best sales quarter. If you'd agree to part-time, you may find working here could generate a story idea. People love to talk at the checkout counter, and I need the help. I'd pay you, of course. Straight commission on anything you sell."

Was she serious? The thought never occurred to Lila. "What happens when I need to return to New York?"

"My mother arrives the week before Christmas. She runs the store like she did her sixth-grade social studies class."

Lila giggled along with Melanie. "That's adorable. I'm sure Aunt Cathy wants to get a few things done in the house, but outside of that, I'm wide open."

"I bet she's in heaven having you home again. She's so proud of you and talks about your books all the time."

A Christmas Kind of Perfect

Lila laid a hand on her chest. "Since Mom and Dad's car accident, she insists her home is mine, too. And I'm glad she's still here in Sister Bay, so I can come back."

"She's often in here buying something for someone. Bless her heart." Melanie twisted her wedding band around her finger. "Well, what do you think about taking the job?"

Lila's gaze drifted to her hands in her lap, as she bought time to think about the offer. Was this the blast of inspiration she needed in her life? "Why not? It could spark an idea for my next book."

Melanie leaned over and grabbed both of Lila's hands and gave a gentle squeeze. "Oh, Lila, you'll come to love it as much as I do. And there's plenty of time to get you trained." Melanie eased back in her chair and fought a yawn. Then she reached under the counter and rummaged and then held out a keychain with a cute lemon drop fob. "Here's my extra key."

Lila took the keychain and slipped off the stool, slipping into her heels. "OK, that's enough for today. You're exhausted." She picked up the plate and her mug.

"Don't you dare clean up. It gives me something to do. But you're right, I'm bushed. Can you come in tomorrow before we open up? It'll give us some time to get started with your training."

Lila reluctantly placed the plate and mug back down on the counter. She grabbed her jacket and purse. "Sure can. I'm so glad I'm here."

"Me, too. Sleep well and we'll meet tomorrow bright and early."

"OK, you too." Lila headed for the door, but not before she gave a quick glance to the back of the room and found Conrad watching her.

Knowing he belonged to someone else now filled her with sorrow…

It was her own fault.

6

Lila pulled into Aunt Cathy's driveway at seven o'clock. An autumn palette of oranges, yellows, and russet browns flanked the side walk. A soft breeze shook loose the remaining leaves overhead from the enormous oak tree Lila had climbed as a child. What a refreshing change from the gray, black, and white tones of Manhattan she'd grown accustomed to. How much she'd missed the colors of the earth. She rang the bell, bringing to life Westminster Abbey chimes.

Her aunt opened the interior door. "Lila, honey, come on in. You don't need to ring the doorbell. You're home."

With those few welcoming words, Lila was reminded of her parents' fatal accident five years ago. She knew their deaths were part of the reason she stayed away for as long as she did—that and her breakup with Conrad. She inhaled and exhaled, coming to terms with their deaths all over again. The hurt finally healed over. The scab had disappeared but a scar remained. She thanked God for her relationship with her aunt, as close to a mother-daughter bond as she would ever have now.

She opened the screen door and stepped into the foyer. Thick arms wrapped around her, and with them came a delicious scent of vanilla. Her aunt was baking again.

Aunt Cathy helped her out of her coat and hung it in the closet. Across the room, family photos lined the staircase wall, beginning with the framed wedding picture Lila remembered so well and the children, whom her aunt referred to as her blessings that followed. Six years had passed since Uncle Ralph died, but his favorite chair and worn footstool remained in the corner of the room. Lila was filled with a sense of comfort missing in her life for a long time.

"I pulled a Dutch apple pie out of the oven about an hour ago and made a batch of your uncle's award-winning chili earlier today. Let's go to the kitchen and enjoy a little supper together."

Lila's stomach growled in agreement. She'd had very little to eat today. She suspected her aunt waited to eat with her, which warmed Lila's heart. She followed Aunt Cathy into the kitchen. "That sounds perfect. I'm starved." Everything remained in the same order as it had been five years before, including the original floral wallpaper, the hurricane lamp in the window, and the oversized cooktop her aunt referred to as "Big Mama."

"Me, too." Her aunt ladled hot chili into a soup tureen. Lila retrieved the bowls from the same maple cabinet that had always housed them, grabbed a couple of soup spoons from the drawer, and joined her aunt at the solid wood kitchen table.

Once seated, Aunt Cathy folded her hands and bowed her head. "Lord, thank You for the food on this table and for Your hand in our lives every single day. In Jesus name we pray."

Lila followed her aunt's lead and mouthed, "Amen." She eyed the meal. "I can't remember the last time I ate chili. It smells delicious."

Aunt Cathy spooned two servings into the bowls. "I remembered how much you liked your uncle's recipe and with a nip in the air I decided to stir up a batch."

"Ah, you couldn't have made a better choice. I'm starved."

Aunt Cathy giggled. "You probably haven't eaten much all day, right?"

Lila smiled. "I had a scone at Window Shopping. It's a lovely store. Melanie has done a fabulous job. I had a difficult time leaving."

"I try to get down there and buy a little something every now and again. Did you notice the area in the store she dedicated to you and your books?"

"Yes, I was surprised."

"She doing OK?" Aunt Cathy furrowed her brow.

"Her back's giving her grief, and she's tired."

"Poor thing. She hired college kids this summer. Are they all gone?"

Lila reached for a napkin. "Back to school I suspect."

"And having no family around makes it tough. She'll need help soon. She won't be able to keep going at this pace—not with twins on the way."

Lila rested an elbow on the table. "Jack wants her to close the store early after Fall Fest."

"I can understand why, but she'd miss out on the Christmas buying season. When her mother visits, she takes over so Melanie gets a break. I help out, but I'm not interested in anything permanent."

"She's asked me to work in the afternoons." Lila allowed the news to percolate. "What do you think?"

"You?" Cathy's eyebrows shot up. "What about the work on your next book?"

Lila tipped her bowl and scooped up the last of her chili on the spoon. "I can handle both, and to be honest, I'm searching for story ideas. Melanie thought working the store might light a spark of inspiration for me."

"She's right. The stories you'll hear will knock your socks off. I love the idea, and you'll catch all the post-festival sales. Most of the other retailers close up and go south for the winter months."

Lila nodded. "It's another way I can help her out."

"Funny how things fall into place, isn't it? Didn't she have a ramp installed for the handicapped? I'm sure that cost her some."

"Conrad's finishing that up."

Aunt Cathy paused. "Conrad?" Her question held a hint of surprise bordering on shock.

Lila shifted in her seat. She half-expected what was coming next.

"You spoke with Conrad. Face-to-face?"

"Um-hmm." Lila bent the edge of the placemat forward and backward between her fingers. "He's going to install a small riser for the signing." Lila wiped her mouth with the napkin.

"How did that go?" Aunt Cathy asked as she ladled a second helping of chili into her bowl. It appeared as if she were settling in for a long discussion as she reseated herself in her chair.

Lila shrugged, ignoring the twinge inside with the mention of her ex-boyfriend. "I think it went well after not talking with each other for the last five years."

"He comes around here from time to time if I need something fixed. With Ralph gone, he's a real blessing. He charges a fair price, and his work is topnotch. And because he's local, folks naturally trust him. Easy on the eyes, too, isn't he?"

Lila fought back a smile. "Don't start, Aunt

Cathy."

Her aunt filled Lila's mug with tea. Before placing the teapot on the table, she refilled her own. "I wondered if you ever sat down with Conrad and talked things through."

Lila hesitated, not wanting to open up old wounds. "It didn't work out for us. He chose to start his business in Sister Bay, and I picked New York. End of story."

"What did you do about the hurt and disappointment?" Aunt Cathy sipped from her mug.

Lila exhaled. "Lived with it, I guess. Our demise seemed to be the casualty for our successes."

"Unresolved issues in life tend to bubble up and reappear later. Remember the days of making applesauce together? I told you how important it was to peel off all of the apple skins before adding them to the pot?"

Lila flashed a smile in her aunt's direction. One of her life lessons was headed in her direction.

Aunt Cathy wiggled a finger in the air to help make her point. "The little bit of skin that you missed made its way into the jars. That's when you realized you failed in making the perfect sauce."

"Where are you going with this?" Lila asked.

"Time has taught me many things. One of them is that unresolved issues in life tend to resurface until you make them right."

Lila placed her spoon on the table. What was her aunt getting at? "I'm here for the book signing to help out Melanie."

"No, that's the issue that brought you home. Maybe you're really here to make it right with Conrad."

"How would I do that? It's pretty clear he's moved on. Melanie told me he's almost engaged, right?" Lila sipped the chamomile tea.

"Yes. That may be true, which means there's not much time left."

Lila stared, open-mouthed, uncertain of her aunt's antics. "What are you up to?" she asked and hoped she wouldn't regret asking it.

Aunt Cathy raised her hand as if halting traffic. "Let me ask you something. What is the last good relationship you've had? And I'm not referring to the one-sided liaisons you've entered into knowing they weren't going anywhere."

Oh no. "I've been dating. Remember the man I met at Stonewood's Halloween party?"

Cathy gave Lila a perturbed glance. "And that lasted how long? Six months? And the one before him, a doctor, right?"

Lila's defenses stirred. "Yes. At first, it was exciting to be with such a confident, well-connected man, but a lifetime of arrogance and self-centeredness?" Lila shook her head. "No, thanks."

"And the actor?" She wiggled her shoulders back and forth in a comical fashion.

Lila stifled a giggle. Her memory was no match for her aunt's. She remembered details about Lila's life that even Lila chose not to remember. "We agreed from the start it was all fun, and we'd never go anywhere."

"My point exactly. Lila, you deliberately choose the wrong man, over and over again. I suspect Conrad's done the same thing, settling for Suzanne."

Lila bent her head, studying her fingers. What could she say to counter her aunt's opinion? Her mind reeled backward in time, searching for proof to weaken her argument. But all she found was evidence against her. The men in her past were one of three things—too young, too vain, or too unavailable. Her aunt won that debate. But was she also right about Conrad?

Aunt Cathy placed a warm hand over Lila's. "Lila, there are no mistakes in life. You and Conrad had something very special, and that doesn't keep coming around in life. Sometimes, that kind of perfect happens only once."

Lila fumbled for words. What could she say? Conrad was taken.

Cathy sliced the pie and served both of them a generous piece. "How's everything in New York? Still all you thought it would be?"

Lila pulled the plate toward her. "I love my career, and the success, but I've paid a huge price for it."

Her aunt waited. "Are you talking about what happened between you and Conrad?"

Lila sunk a fork into the pie. Creamy, cinnamon-speckled apples spread across her plate. "Among other things."

"Like?"

Lila stared at her plate. "I didn't realize how much I've missed home. New York is full of brand-new opportunities all the time, but it's not home—the place where you're understood. The tiny corner of the world where nothing can harm you. It's safe and warm and the place where you can lay your head on a pillow and fall asleep to the sound of crickets instead of sirens and traffic and noise."

Lila lifted her gaze.

Her aunt smiled at her.

"And I was beginning to think you'd never learn." She stood and started to clear away the dishes.

7

Lila parked the car in the store's back lot, next to a large red Hamilton Construction truck. She rubbed the back of her neck. *He* was here.

She fished around in her purse for the lemon drop keychain Melanie gave her last night. It slid into the lock easily. She gave the handle a slight lift and a quick turn with the passkey and pushed hard. A gust of air swooshed into the foyer, causing stacked laminate flooring to topple over and cascade over the floor like a can of pickup sticks. She pressed her hand against her chest.

Lila shrieked. "Oh, my! Look what I've done."

Conrad peeked around the corner, his eyebrows pinched together. "Careful where you walk now."

"I am so sorry. Let me help." Lila placed her purse on the floor and began to pick up her end of the floorboards. Conrad held up his side.

"Remember when we stacked wood in your uncle's shop?" The words spilled out as she laid the last of the boards back in place on the pile.

Conrad snickered. "What I remember is waiting on you to do your half of the work."

"Me, the dead weight? I think not." Lila scrambled to fill the silence that ensued after she alluded to a joke they used to share. "Melanie speaks highly of your company."

He gave her a curt nod. "Good to hear."

"When did you start it up?"

"About four years ago."

"And your brother Luke? Is he part of the company, too?"

"Part-time only, until we get bigger. He went to work for an engineering company down in Sturgeon Bay right after college. Cassie helps out keeping things straight in the office."

Lila's mouth fell open. "Cassie? She was still in high school the last time I saw her."

Conrad shrugged. "A lot has changed over the years. I was a little surprised to learn you were coming back for a book signing. I wouldn't think a career as big as yours could afford time off."

With one sentence, a barrier sprung up between them. The awkward silence lingered like a dense fog that wouldn't clear.

"Listen, sorry again about the mess I caused. I'd better get over by Mel." She walked alongside the yellow tape that guided her footsteps.

"Don't forget this."

Lila turned back around to find Conrad holding her purse. In another time, or under different circumstances, it would make a funny sight. Instead, she reached for the bag.

Their hands brushed against each other. Lila took in a quick breath to still the charge that raced through her, the power of his touch igniting an inner spark.

He narrowed his eyes. "Were you running this morning?"

Lila grinned and lifted one shoulder. "I'm a little out of practice, but it was exhilarating. I can't remember the last time I went out for a run."

He hooked his hammer into his toolbelt. "I can relate. It's been too long since I've taken a decent hike. I used to love that."

"I remember." Lila looked at the floor and then back up at him.

"Lila, is that you?" Melanie's voice sang out.

"I guess duty calls." Lila thumbed to the front of the store.

He gave her a slight tilt of his head. "You'd better move along, or she'll come down here."

Her gaze lingered on him for a minute. She wished things were different between them. She turned and walked to the front of the store.

Melanie stood behind the checkout counter. "Good morning. I confess I'm excited for today." She placed her purse on the shelf under the counter and moved to stand beside her friend.

Darkness circled Melanie's eyes.

"Have you slept?" Lila brushed her hand across Melanie's back.

"The boys kicked and played like crazy. When I don't sleep well, neither does Jack. His soft heart seems to double in size where I'm concerned. Conrad was like that with you too. Remember?"

Lila nodded. She'd lost count of the number of times she caught Conrad giving something up so she could benefit. If there were two places they had to be at the same time, he'd often feign disinterest to his and default to her preference. Or he'd agree to do things most men would not want to do, like singing in the Christmas choir at church. Those attributes were hard to find in a man, and if anybody learned that, it was Lila.

Melanie walked over to the display window.

Lila followed.

"I love this corner of the store because of the natural light. When the days grow shorter, as they are now, I use hidden rope lighting to keep the area lit. I'd like to turn the window decorations over to you, starting today. It's getting more difficult to set up and take down the props."

Lila nodded. "No problem, I'd love to."

"It takes a lot of imagination to come up with enticing displays to draw the customer into the store. I'm sure you'll be good at it."

Lila imagined all kinds of possibilities. "Now I understand why you want the riser placed here. It's perfect."

"We need to accommodate the audience members outside as well as inside."

Lila straightened a stack of devotionals on a nearby table, forming an attractive domino layout. "You still think we'll get a packed house?"

"I do. You're a living, breathing success story for Sister Bay."

Lila sighed, unsure how to handle the attention and praise. She'd paid a high price for her achievements, but had she made the right choice for her life?

The rest of the morning flew by as they devised a timetable for the book signing. They covered the floorplan, the presentation, the reading, checkout procedures, and the refreshments they planned to offer.

When they finished the training, Melanie crossed her arms. "What are you doing for the rest of the day?"

"I'm wide open. Do you need some help with something?" Lila slid the scissor in the direction of the tape dispenser and took mental note of the remaining gift wrap on a large spool.

"I'd like to show you my routine for the

afternoons since you'll be taking them over."

Lila brought her hands together. Finally, she'd be able to do something to help Melanie. "Sounds good to me. Let's get busy."

"First off, I could use some help in the kitchen. I need to stir up a batch of cranberry scones. We'll offer them at the signing."

Baking was not part of her skill set. She took a deep breath, garnering up her courage, and followed Melanie toward the kitchen in the back of the store. They passed Conrad, who was nailing sideboards onto the ramp.

"Are you headed where I think you are?" He held the hammer in midair, looked toward the kitchen and back to her, mock horror on his face.

Lila stifled a giggle, shrugged, and crossed her fingers.

He winced.

She'd show him. How hard could it be to make scones? She followed Melanie into the kitchen, which was small but well-equipped. Of course, Lila's frame of reference was limited. Everything appeared in order. Muffin and bread pans hung from baker's hooks on a large pegboard. An enormous mixer was positioned in a corner on the countertop. A stainless-steel side-by-side refrigerator stood like a sentry guarding the room. A farmhouse style sink, a gas cooktop, and double ovens lined the opposite wall. A five-foot working island overpowered the room, its bottom shelf stacked with a variety of large bowls, pots and pans, mixing cups, and unfamiliar utensils.

Melanie handed her a white chef's apron and put her own on. She tied a loose bow behind her and motioned Lila to do the same.

"It'll take me a minute to slide the afternoon tray into the oven. After that, we'll get started on tomorrow's batch." Melanie walked over to the refrigerator.

Lila slipped the apron on and created a loose knot like Melanie's behind her back. "What if customers walk into the store?"

Melanie pointed up to the ceiling's corner. "I installed a small intercom device for that purpose."

Lila rested a hand on her chest. "Good thinking."

"Actually, it was Jack's idea. He's familiar with how I can slip into another world when I get into a kitchen."

Lila's phone buzzed in her back pocket. She tugged it out.

Andrea's smiling face filled the display, but Lila allowed the call to go to her voicemail. She'd contact her agent later.

"Everything OK? You can take that call." Melanie pulled some bowls out from under the counter.

"No, I don't need to. Now let's get busy with that recipe of yours. I'm actually excited to bake." She dropped the phone into the apron's pocket and pushed up the sleeves of her cashmere sweater.

"OK, if you say so. Now I'm going to share with you my secret to a perfect scone. You don't overwork the dough. It's similar to making a pie crust or a batch of biscuits." Melanie lifted a full pound block of butter from the refrigerator, wrapped in wax paper.

Lila sighed. My goodness that was a lot of butter and Melanie's reference to pie dough fell on deaf ears. Should she confess that she'd never made a pie, much less her own crust?

"What's the matter? You look like you did when

Mrs. Warren told us we were having a pop quiz."

Lila grimaced. "It's the baking. I haven't done much in the last decade."

"For me, it's something fun to do. What do you do when you're not working?"

"I get together with friends. Once a month we go out for dinner and let our hair down."

"Sounds nice. I need to do more of that myself. Good old-fashioned girl fun. But what happens on regular nights of the week?"

Lila shrugged. "You can buy whatever your heart desires in Manhattan from the small vendors or bakery cafés. There's really no need to be in the kitchen when everything you could ever want is right out your front door."

Melanie rolled up her sleeves. "Wow, I can't imagine. Well, you're not in New York anymore. Here we work the dough with our own two hands."

Lila widened her eyes as if she won the first prize at the county fair for one of her entries.

The two women cackled. "Listen to me. If you can write one bestseller after another, this will be a piece of Door County cherry pie. I make a double batch every night. One tray goes out in the morning and the other midafternoon. What we're doing today is dedicated to the signing."

Conrad walked by and stopped in the doorway, finishing up a conversation on his phone. Despite his furrowed brow, his tone was calm and reassuring. "I'll be there in an hour."

He most likely made the promise constantly. He was raised to stand behind his word. He had to have carried that trait over into his business.

"Ladies, the ramp is done. I need to get to an

appointment, but I'll be back later tonight to put up the riser." He wrapped three times on the doorframe, signaling his departure, but before he left, he turned to lock eyes with Lila's.

"Good luck with the scones." Conrad gave Lila a thumbs-up.

"Conrad, you've got your key, right?" Melanie asked.

He wiggled a lemon drop chain similar to the one Melanie had given Lila. "Yup. I'll make sure to lock up."

Melanie placed her hands on her rounded hips. "Thanks so much, Conrad."

"Don't mention it," he said and turned from the doorway.

A moment later, the door closed behind him.

"Busy guy, huh?" Lila was curious about the man who once stole her heart.

Melanie sighed. "Unbelievably so. He never stops, and he doesn't have someone special keeping an eye on him. Not like you used to do."

"I thought he and Suzanne were almost engaged."

"According to her they are, but sometimes I wonder about them. She's devoted to her career. That seems to come first, even before Conrad. She won some kind of Realtor of the Year award last year, and with his line of work, he's no better. They're down at Al Johnson's place quite a bit. I often wonder if Conrad's thinking about what kind of home life that would be for him? And how do kids fit in? Conrad's always talked like he wanted a houseful of kids."

8

Lila was bone tired when she pulled into Aunt Cathy's driveway. She was used to the exhaustion that came after a frustrating day working out one of her stubborn scenes. A cup of her favorite blend of chamomile tea with a little honey helped her unwind with that type of tired. This kind needed a hot meal, a bubble bath, and a good-night's sleep.

Lila parked the car and started up the walk. She'd been so busy all day that she'd forgotten to check for any other calls other than the one she'd received earlier. She patted her back pocket and then reached into her purse—nothing. Later in the day, they'd changed the sign on the window to add Lila's number in case of an emergency at the store. And Melanie would surely have Jack call her if she went into early labor. She needed that phone. She was so close to the door now. She wanted to reach out and turn the knob and walk in.

The apron.

She exhaled, realizing what she must do. Retracing her steps, she slid back into the car, slipped the gear into reverse, and headed back to the store.

Conrad's truck was parked outside. A man of his word, he was working to complete Melanie's task as promised. A task light illuminated his finished work. The riser, complete with a short set of stairs, was placed in front of the display window, exactly where Melanie wanted it.

Conrad stood in the shadows, holding his hammer

like a guitar. He stepped to the beat of one of their favorite songs. Lila slowed her steps, not wanting to ruin the moment. An ache, years old, filled her. A beat-up boom box sat on the floor, thumping the tune.

Lila closed her eyes, instantly transported to the past, sitting next to Conrad in his old pickup, his hand resting on her knee. They'd gone down to Sturgeon Bay to a movie.

He pulled up alongside the curb in front of her house and shifted the vehicle into park. The only light came from a street lamp on the corner. He turned toward her and slipped his arm around her shoulders. She watched his eyes move up her body and pause on her lips. "Lila." He breathed her name with such tenderness she had trouble believing her ears over the beat of her own heart. Thick, dark lashes hooded his dark eyes. The boyish grin, the one she'd become so accustomed to, was replaced with luminous parted lips.

The clang of metal—a hammer into a toolbox—startled her thoughts bringing her back to the present. She blinked and shuddered at the sound.

Conrad shifted in her direction. "Hey, there. I didn't expect anyone tonight. Sorry if I scared you."

"Hey, there, yourself. I never thought you'd be here so late."

He tilted his head toward the front of the store. "The riser needed to get up. I don't want Melanie worrying about anything in the state she's in."

Lila walked in the direction of the riser. "You laid it out perfectly. Mel wanted to make it possible for her customers outside to get a glimpse of what's going on inside. She expects a packed house. I hope, for her sake, that's exactly what happens." She bent over and joined Conrad picking up the scattered tools.

"It wouldn't surprise me if it was a standing-room-only crowd. I'm sure you're quite the draw for Sister Bay. A lot of folks are proud of you."

Did that include him? "I'm not sure I believe that, but I'm here and I'll do my best."

"Do you have anyone special coming to the event? Friends, maybe a boyfriend, that you might like to reserve seating?"

Lila grabbed the broom and began sweeping up wood shavings from the floor. "No one. Aunt Cathy, maybe. Otherwise, I don't have a boyfriend. I got close once or twice to having something—" she paused for lack of words "—permanent, but for one reason or another it didn't work out. Wasn't meant to be, I guess. And you?" If what Melanie told her was true about his relationship with Suzanne nearing marriage, she wanted him to tell her. After the hurt she'd caused him, she deserved whatever he told her.

He closed the toolbox and secured the latch. "Dated pretty serious with a flight attendant for a few years, but that wasn't right. In the end, we realized we weren't a good fit." He lifted his shoulders. "I'm not the most exciting guy around. When Suzanne came along, well—" his eyes focused on his boots—"things changed up again." He positioned the dust pan for her, and she swept the contents from the floor into the pan. A thick pause settled between them.

Lila wished she'd come home long ago. Perhaps everything would be different for both of them.

He cleared his throat. "She's expecting a ring this Christmas." His words hung in the air.

She fought the desire to reach out and caress his shoulders or to wipe the wood shavings from his hair.

"Well, she's a lucky lady if that happens."

Conrad shrugged. "So, what brings you back here tonight?"

Lila headed for the kitchen, fighting a rise of jealousy evoked by his news. Why shouldn't Conrad propose? She didn't expect him to stay single forever. Or had she? "I forgot my phone. I think I left it in the apron pocket."

She entered the dark kitchen and slid her hand up the wall, searching for the light switch. It all looked so different in the dark. A real sense of agitation filled her. Her nerves were as raw as the shredded jalapenos she'd worked with earlier today.

He was close. His cologne so fragrant of the earth and wind. It swirled around her leaving her lightheaded. He moved and settled right behind her, the heat from his body intoxicating her. His breath on her neck weakening her knees. Old familiar tingles shot up her spine. Her breath now jagged. Seconds ticked like rapid fire on the wall clock. His rough, callused hand covered hers. His touch reminded her how things once were between them. Together, they flipped up the switch. A click. A sputter. And the fluorescent bulbs overhead bathed the kitchen in jarring light. The moment gone.

He backed away.

Lila swallowed hard in an attempt to slow her racing heart. She didn't have to see her reflection in a mirror. Her face and neck had to be as red as a June rose petal.

He gave her a quick nod and a smile she'd like to gift wrap for herself. "There you be."

She returned a nervous smile back at him and wished something would distract his attention from her unease.

His eyes locked in on hers.

For a moment, Lila feared he understood what passed between them. He thumbed in the direction of the front of the store. "I'll be up front unless you need some help finding that phone."

"No. I mean yes. Go ahead. I'll be fine." Grateful for his turned back, she laid a hand on her chest to steady her heart. Her breathing began to slow. Melanie told herself he was almost an engaged man, but that didn't seem to bear any weight. His power over her was as strong as ever. What was she thinking? Whatever it was, she'd better stop it right now. Get ahold of her emotions.

Thankful for somewhere to go with her raging adrenaline, she fished the apron out of the soiled laundry bin and slipped her hand into the deep pocket. Sure enough, her phone was there. She hit the power button and the phone whistled its tune. The voice messaging icon blinked, reminding her of Andrea's call along with five unanswered text messages. She sighed, turned off the lights, and headed outside. She found Conrad packing up his truck.

Conrad peeked his head out from behind his truck. "Any luck?"

Lila raised the phone. "Right in the apron pocket where I left it."

"How would we manage without them?"

The expression on his face told her he didn't expect an answer.

"I'd like to find out," she added and wondered if there were times he'd agree.

He tilted his head in surprise. "By the way, I'm praying for you to have a great book signing."

Lila fished for her keys in her purse pocket. "Thanks. Will your mother be coming?"

"She wouldn't miss it. I'll be bringing her. Dad's got bowling, and Cassie has a date. So that leaves me."

"What about Luke?"

"Luke? A wife and two kids under five keep him pretty busy."

Lila gasped as she walked to her vehicle. "Two kids. I bet they're adorable."

"They are. He always wanted a big family." He spoke with the pride of a father and not that of an uncle.

"You did, too, if I remember correctly." Lila bit her lip, regretting the dredging up of the past.

Clunk. He slammed the tailgate closed. "Yup, you're right, once upon a time, I did. I'm not sure the idea of having kids is part of Suzanne's plan for us, though. She's starting to make an impact in real estate, and I'm in the same position. We may end up as, what do people call them, DINKS?"

Lila snickered at the reference. "Dual income, no kids." But as the words left her lips, she was certain the acronym didn't fit him. He'd make a wonderful father, and they realized that a long time ago. Lila wondered what other dreams had died for Conrad.

He knocked the top of his truck hood three times, signaling the end of the conversation. "I'll lock up. Good night, Lila."

She opened her car door. "Good night, Conrad. I hope you're headed home. You've put in a hard day's work."

On her way back to Aunt Cathy's, Lila reached for her phone and decided to call Andrea. No answer. She left a brief message, told her everything was on schedule, and she'd call again in a few days after the signing. Guilt rippled up her back as she realized she was lying to Andrea in that voicemail. She was no closer to an idea for her next book than she was before leaving New York.

9

Conrad loved Lila's suggestion to go home to a hot shower and a good meal. Instead, he drove down to Al Johnson's, gave his hair a quick comb, and headed into the restaurant. He found Suzanne sitting at their usual table by the window.

He pulled out his chair and sat, taking his menu in hand, even though he didn't need one. Their competing schedules had them eating here several times a week.

Suzanne placed her menu on the table, signaling the waitress they were ready to order. "How was your day? Mine was crazy busy. Two closings this morning, and in the afternoon, Bud came into my office and closed the door. He started in again about the Madison—"

A young woman approached their table. "Are you ready to order?"

Despite his good manners, Conrad ordered first. He wanted to avoid the glare Suzanne was sure to give the waitress for interrupting the conversation, one of Suzanne's pet peeves. "Yes, we are. I'd like the Swedish meatball plate," he said. He avoided Suzanne's gaze in the process, since she didn't appreciate poor etiquette either.

Suzanne glanced up at the waitress, "Chef's salad, dressing on the side. I'd like a cup of hot water with lemon, too, please. Thank you."

Conrad sighed. The brew Suzanne ordered would

curb her appetite. Was it so difficult to splurge once and eat a decent meal?

The waitress reached for the menus. "Of, course. I'll get those out to you right away."

Conrad placed his hand over Suzanne's and peered into the eyes that made him forget about Lila and the hurt from the past.

"You've got that devilish grin again," she whispered after the waitress placed her hot water brew on the table.

She flashed him an irresistible smile that encouraged him to pull her into the corner and kiss her. Instead, he brought her hand to his lips. "So, you were telling me about your day."

Suzanne's face lit up as if she was the recipient of a surprise party. "I may be up for the Realtor of the Year award again. Can you believe that?"

She worked sixty-plus hours a week, covered the county for showings and open houses, and told him she usually didn't get home until after eight on most nights. No one else was more dedicated or invested in the business.

"No, it doesn't surprise me at all. I appreciate how much effort and dedication you put into your job, and I'm proud of you. I hope that means that same passion will slide over into family life one day."

Suzanne withdrew her hand and sat back in her chair as if he'd pushed her. Her beautiful face clouded with distaste as if she bitten into the wedge of lemon floating around in her water. It surprised him. Seconds dragged on. Would she cause a scene?

She steepled her fingers, the tips of her red-painted nails meeting at the points. "A person doesn't work as hard as I do to give it all up down the road.

You need to understand that. There's a window of opportunity in this business, and if you don't jump, you lose. I've always set the highest standards for myself for a reason. This isn't some game I'm playing until we settle down with a house and a bunch of kids."

Conrad tensed, already regretting his mention of a family.

"You may not be aware but there are a lot of men in the world today who choose to give up their careers to become stay-at-home dads."

This was not how Conrad wanted the conversation to go. She never respected the business he'd built. He willed himself to remain quiet.

"Being a handyman—" she lifted her shoulders as if to soften the blow "—well, it's ordinary work."

Conrad bristled. The appetite he'd brought to the restaurant faded. He wrestled with a hard knot in the pit of his stomach. "Handyman? Is that what you think I am?"

Heads turned from neighboring tables, cautioning Conrad to keep his voice in check. He stretched his neck from the tight-fitting collar of the shirt he wished he changed. "Where are you going with this? You've always understood my business."

"Well, aren't you helping out your friend Melanie again?" she whispered the question in an endearing tone, but Conrad sensed the malice beneath the words.

He enjoyed her sarcastic sense of humor, so different from his own, but tonight her vindictive nature was aimed in his direction. The job with Melanie bothered her.

"I accepted Melanie's job because I promised her years ago, I'd be there for her. She helped me out when

I was new and starting out. You are aware that her husband travels a lot and is rarely home."

Suzanne furrowed her brows. "You keep doing little jobs like that one for your friend, and you'll end up building the wrong reputation. Dad says you should let all that go and focus more on big contract jobs with Peninsula Homes."

Conrad hated that she spoke to her father about his business. They went over that topic more than once, yet she couldn't seem to refrain from sharing every detail with him.

"I don't need your father's advice when it comes to my occupation. The man is a retired teacher. No offense, but he doesn't have the background or experience to run a business-like mine."

Conrad exhaled and with his hands clasped together, he clenched them tightly. He had trouble following her logic. She might be smart in real estate negotiations, but he wondered about her priorities in life.

The waitress approached the table with a large serving platter hoisted on a shoulder. "Here we go. I've got a chef's salad and a Swedish meatball plate."

Suzanne ignored the waitress as she served the salad and Conrad's entrée. "By the way, isn't your old girlfriend in town? I couldn't help but notice the posters splattered in every store window in the village. Did you run into her yet?" Suzanne asked.

Conrad focused on the dinner in front of him. He didn't want this conversation to turn from bad to ugly, but the hurricane in his gut told him it was already too late. He picked up his knife and fork and began slicing one of the meatballs. "Yeah, we had a meeting together." He slid a piece of a meatball in his mouth, hoping his answer satisfied her.

She lowered her fork. "When?"

He wiped his mouth before answering. "I was finishing up the exit ramp. Lila was in the store, so Melanie called me over to discuss erecting a riser for the book signing. End of story."

"Riser?" Suzanne hissed. "Good grief. Most authors stand behind a podium. She requested a riser?"

Conrad allowed his fork to drop onto his plate with a clang. "She didn't ask for a riser. Melanie suggested it so everyone could get a glimpse of her. It's a small store and Melanie expects a packed house."

"You sure seem well-informed."

Conrad exhaled a frustrated sigh—the classical music playing in the background doing little to calm his nerves. "I'm the contractor. That's it. Why do you insist on needling me at the end of a day?"

Suzanne acted as if his question was never asked. "I don't plan on going to that event. I never cared for her books anyway."

Conrad couldn't remember the last time Suzanne read a book.

She slid her half-eaten salad to the side and wiped her full lips with the paper napkin from her lap. "You're not going either, are you?"

He narrowed his eyes and gestured for a moment. He leaned back from his plate and swallowed down his food. "I need to take Mom. Dad's bowling and Cassie's got a date."

"You need to or want to?"

Conrad scowled. He wolfed down his dinner at the tempo of his accelerating heart and was certain he'd later pay for it with indigestion. "I'm not letting my mother down. She's read everything Lila's written, and she wants to go to the signing. Like everyone else in the village, you're aware this is a big event. Why all the questions? It's not like I expect to track you down every minute of the day and night."

"I'd say it's a bit different, isn't it, Conrad? You're attending your old girlfriend's book signing. What kind of impression is that going to make with everyone?"

"I'm taking my mother to an event everyone in Door County, except you, will be attending. I don't think it's going to rock anyone's world or look out of place at all. Aren't you overreacting a little? What's this all about?"

Suzanne wore the pout of a young child. "First you tell me you want me to give up my career and now you're planning to go to your ex-girlfriend's book signing. How do you think I'm supposed to react? I thought we'd share a nice dinner tonight, and it's turned out miserably. I'm beginning to wonder if I was wrong choosing to ignore my father's advice when he told me to be wary of you."

He gazed at Suzanne with a new perspective. She would never give up her career.

They may as well have been eating alone as the silence stretched between them.

When he finished his meal, he leaned forward. "Where do you see us in five years?"

With her elbows resting on the table, she laced her pretty fingers and rested a delicate chin on them. Once, he thought he'd never tire of staring at her beautiful face. "Well, I hope to be running my own agency with a large staff of realtors working for me. To be honest, my goal is to be recognized as the largest real estate company in the county. After that, I'd like to franchise throughout the state."

Everything was about her—about her career, her desires. She gave no thought to what he'd have to give up: children, his business, his self-esteem. He shook his head.

"All finished here?" the waitress asked, laying the bill facedown.

Conrad put his napkin on the table, picked up the bill, and held out his hand to Suzanne. "Yes. Yes. I believe we're quite finished."

10

Conrad followed Suzanne down the aisle of the grocery store. Their silent parting during their previous dinner must have left her thinking about what she'd said. She'd actually offered to cook dinner for him tonight. Otherwise, he wouldn't be with her now.

In the middle of the condiment aisle, he leaned to kiss her cheek.

"Don't you dare," Suzanne shrieked.

"Why not?"

Suzanne smoothed her hair. "Someone may see you. I have a reputation to uphold." She pressed her hands on his chest, a maneuver to keep him at a distance. "Now go find us a nice bottle of sparkling water for dinner."

He took five minutes to make his choice and retrace his steps. He was making his way back to her, but stopped midstride when he noticed his mother approaching Suzanne, who was waiting at the meat counter. He stepped behind a kiosk, choosing not to interrupt the two women and anticipated a cute exchange between them.

"Suzanne, is that you?" his mother asked.

Conrad sighed. Suzanne kept her back to his mother long enough for him to notice, the discontent prickling up his neck. He always hoped—no he prayed—that their relationship would be similar to the one Lila always had with his mom—one so close that it resembled a mother and daughter.

Suzanne finally turned to face Mom. Conrad recognized her realtor 'work' smile. He noticed it many times when their paths crossed in their professional lives. She made no attempt to embrace his mother. Isn't that what women usually did instinctively, especially with family? Instead, Suzanne didn't move. "How are you Mrs. Hamilton?"

"Well, I'm fine and dandy, but it's been way too long since you've come around. You and Conrad should have dinner with us one of these Sundays."

"That sounds like a lovely idea."

"By the way, did you happen to notice the Christmas decorations this year? I think the decision to purchase the extra-large bells was a good one, don't you?"

Conrad's heart gave a tug. It would be so like his mother to comment on the new decorations. Suzanne smiled down at his mother but said nothing.

His mother took a step toward Suzanne and touched her forearm. The gesture was uniquely his mother's, working to draw people toward her tenderness and compassion.

"Will you be joining Conrad and me for Lila's book signing tomorrow night?"

Conrad held his breath. He hoped Suzanne knew better than to open up with his mother on that issue. Suzanne could be flat out unpredictable. A trait he often found entertaining when they were with their friends, but it wouldn't be cute today with his mother.

Suzanne accepted the package from the butcher and turned back to Conrad's mother. "I'm not certain, but I think everyone in the village is going to the event."

Conrad released his breath.

His mother flashed one of her 'I've got a secret' smiles.

Conrad couldn't help but snicker.

"Rumor has it that some folks are driving over as far away as Appleton. It should be a good crowd."

His mother would be in the loop about the signing. Although she blamed Lila for hurting him, she would always harbor a soft spot for Lila in her heart.

"Seems Lila can still draw a crowd," Suzanne said.

"Oh, yes, indeed. I think she has a loyal following, including me." Mom rested a finger alongside her face.

When Suzanne's smart phone rang, Conrad stepped forward. "Well hello, Mom. Funny finding you here."

His mother startled. She laid a hand on her chest. "I could say the same about you," kissing his cheek.

"I'm going to have to take this call," Suzanne said.

Conrad nodded, and Suzanne turned her back to them, her phone to her ear.

"I was telling Suzanne that you need to bring her over to the house after church one Sunday. Let me know, and I'll make a nice pot roast. The one you like with the little red potatoes and carrots."

"I will, Mom, and soon."

"OK, dear, I need to run. Your father's waiting for supper, and you remember how grumpy he can be when he gets hungry."

Conrad smiled, hoping Suzanne would care for him the same way in the future. "You go ahead. I'll tell Suzanne good-bye for you."

"Love you, dear. I'm excited for tomorrow night."

Conrad gave her a quick wink. "Me, too. Drive

safe."

She waved a good-bye and wheeled her cart down the coffee aisle.

Suzanne slid her phone back into the leather purse on her arm. "It was Bud, reminding me of our meeting tomorrow." She huffed.

"Oh." Conrad sighed. "Do we have everything we need?"

Suzanne nodded and Conrad walked at her side as they made their way toward the front of the store.

"Is Bud still the go-getter in the office?"

"Oh, yes. He's making plans for something big down the road."

Conrad wasn't impressed. He'd met Bud once a few months ago at an after-hours event hosted by the Chamber. The man was mouthy, bragged about the big deals he was making, and referred to Suzanne as his rising star.

"Mom wants me to bring you by after church one of these Sundays."

Suzanne placed the potatoes and asparagus onto the conveyer belt. "Did you tell her we don't go to church?"

"I'll save that conversation for later." He lifted his work boot and set it on the carriage of the cart.

"Hmm, I thought so. At least we still have that in common, don't we?" she said with a devious smile.

Conrad agreed with a shrug, but he hated to admit it. "I'll get the truck and meet you out front." He turned for the door leaving Suzanne to empty what remained in the cart.

11

The day of the book signing Lila and Melanie rearranged the store—Lila doing all of the heavy work while Melanie rested on a stool behind the counter. They dressed out the riser with a multicolored hook rug, a steamer trunk filled with afghans, and tapestry pillows. Lila's books, framed reviews, and posters were arranged in a wooden bookcase. The rope lighting outlined the display window, providing an ethereal touch. Lila preferred a more intimate setting for the audience and chose a stool for her seating.

After positioning her books behind the counter, Lila checked her watch. In an hour, their first guests would arrive. She walked into the kitchen to find Melanie topping off the last tray of scones with a thick almond icing.

Lila brought her hands together. "The scones are so festive. The red in the cranberries and the green jalapeños shout, 'Christmas is coming!'"

"I bet you never expected to enjoy baking. I told you so." Melanie beamed like a new teacher in a classroom. She rubbed at her back with both hands and winced in pain.

Lila sighed not sure what to do for her friend. She grabbed a nearby chair and slid it over to where Melanie stood. "You OK? Sit down a minute and put your feet up."

"I haven't told Jack yet, but I've been having Braxton Hicks for the past couple of weeks."

Lila rolled her eyes. "What are Braxton Hicks?"

Melanie giggled. "Lila, there's so much ahead of you. Braxton Hicks are weak contractions before the real ones. When it happened the first time, I panicked. I called my doctor and told him my labor was starting, but he settled me down and explained it was normal. I guess it's the way our body prepares for birth, like a prologue in one of your books."

"Ah, thanks for putting it into my language. I pray I'm as lucky as you one day, expecting my first baby."

Melanie's eyes softened. "If that's what you really want, you can make it happen. But you need the right man by your side. There are some women who decide to go it alone, but we value the same things in life. Having someone who will support you and be there for you in the good moments and the tough ones is important. Jack and I understand we're facing a lot of challenges when we bring the twins home, but we've been preparing for it."

Lila bit her bottom lip. "Sometimes I think my priorities are out of whack, and I've been chasing a hollow dream."

"Your dreams weren't hollow, but they can change. If you're open to it, something you never imagined happening, a new dream better than the one before, may come along. There's always time for that to happen."

Melanie was right. "I need more of your influence in my life. I haven't been this happy in a very long time. And I don't want us to ever drift apart again. I want us to stay as close as we are now."

Melanie stood. "Well, I'm not going anywhere soon, so don't worry about that. Now, let's get you out of that apron and ready for your signing."

12

Conrad slipped behind the wheel of his pickup and followed the car in front of him a little too closely as he tore down the street toward his mother's. The last event he'd thought he'd find himself attending was Lila's book signing. The fact that Suzanne wasn't happy about it didn't help ease Conrad's mind, either. He recalled a bitter argument between them the night before when he dropped Suzanne off after another strained dinner at Al Johnson's.

"You're still in love with her, aren't you?" Suzanne reminded him of one of his nephews refusing to get ready for bed.

"Don't be ridiculous. It's late and you're tired." It wouldn't surprise him if she finished off the evening with a major argument especially after their miserable dinner.

"Aren't you worried about what our friends will say if you dump me for her?"

Conrad slammed his palms against the steering wheel. "I'm not dumping you. Where is this going?"

"I've waited long enough. If we don't make us permanent...."

He interrupted her. "What is this, an ultimatum?"

"I'm not sure how much longer I'm willing to wait for a ring." Without allowing him to answer, she flew open the car door and slammed it shut behind her.

He watched her walk to her apartment and let herself in. She was right. She'd waited long enough.

Conrad cleared his thoughts of Suzanne, and tried to focus on making the evening to turn out special for his mother.

He found Mom waiting for him in the foyer, her tweed coat buttoned up to her neck, hat and gloves in place, her leather purse on her arm.

He winked at her. "Oh, boy. You are ready to go, aren't you?"

"You of all people should know I don't want to be late for anything. I'm not planning on starting now at my age."

"The truck is waiting," Conrad said as if he were the coachman to Cinderella's carriage. He walked his mother to the passenger side of his vehicle.

A few minutes later, they were both seated comfortably in the cab of his pickup. Conrad made it a habit to lift his foot off the gas and slow his speed whenever she rode with him, and tonight was no exception.

"I want to thank you for taking me to this event."

"There's no need, Mom. I enjoy spending time with you. I'm sorry I haven't been over more. I'm doing my best to get my outdoor projects buttoned up before the snow flies."

"I understand how busy you are, and that's why I appreciate it."

Conrad reached over and gave his mom's hand a squeeze.

"This is certainly special, going out with my son."

Conrad made a mental note to spend more time with his mom. He was aware nights like this meant a lot to her. "Me too, Mom."

"Cassie told me you ran into Lila at the store. How did it go?"

Conrad cracked the window, thankful for the rush of cold air that hit him square in the face. "OK, I guess. You can imagine how those things usually turn out."

"Running in to her again couldn't be easy for you. A mother doesn't forget that sort of thing."

"I wouldn't say it was difficult with her."

"Oh?"

Conrad turned the corner "We split on good terms. She went after her dreams. I followed mine."

"You make it sound so simple. I wish I adopted that perspective with all the problems that come my way in life."

Conrad turned on the radio to the country station his mother enjoyed.

"Any old feelings coming back?"

Conrad pulled in a slow breath. His mother always possessed the ability to read him. "To be honest, I'm not sure they ever left. When I first saw her, it was as if five years never passed. I didn't think it possible after how things ended."

"It was always easy with Lila, wasn't it?"

He hid a sigh. No point arguing the truth. "Yeah, it was."

She pressed a light touch on his forearm. "Is she married?"

Conrad turned his eyes off the road for a fraction of a second to throw her a sideways glance. "What?"

His mother raised her voice an octave as if he were hard of hearing. "Is Lila married?"

"No."

"*Hmpf.*"

"What?" This can of worms was better left closed.

"Well, you'd think you'd want to know why."

"She told me she got close a couple of times to something permanent but it didn't pan out. Why? What does that matter now? It's over between us."

His mother's silence was almost worse than her opinion.

"You do realize how close I am to proposing to Suzanne, right?"

"And you understand my concern with that idea. Has she mastered frying a decent egg for your breakfast yet?"

Conrad fought back a chuckle. "I almost regret telling that story to you with how often you bring it up."

"For goodness' sake, if a woman can't make an egg over easy there's not much hope for more."

"Ah, you've got to cut Suzanne some slack. She wasn't raised for cooking and cleaning."

"Or bearing children? How's that little conversation coming along?"

Conrad groaned. She'd hit a nerve. Man, he hoped the evening didn't turn south.

"I'm sorry. Suzanne's a fine woman, headstrong, determined, comes from a good family, and very attractive. I can understand how you'd be drawn to her. I only hope you really think this through before proposing, because that's for life, and this visit from Lila is—"

Conrad scowled. "—Is?"

"A second chance."

"I can't expect that after how I handled things and what I did to her."

"What in heaven's name did *you* do?"

Conrad pulled into the parking lot at Window

Shopping, slid into a stall, and cut the engine. The cab went dark. "It's what I didn't do that's unforgiveable."

His mother's lips turned down at the corners. "Oh, Conrad, you must forgive yourself for whatever wrong you think you committed."

He threw her a weak smile. "I'm working on it, Mom. Now, how about we go in and enjoy this book signing?"

13

Lila recognized some of the faces while others were brand-new to her. As Melanie predicted, the store was packed in thirty minutes. The energy from the audience filled the room like helium in a balloon

Lila stood with Melanie behind the counter and whispered into Melanie's ear. "I think our rearranging earlier was a success."

Melanie beamed. "I told you there would be a standing-room-only crowd if you came, and I was right."

Melanie understood her business. She was an impressive woman and a true entrepreneur.

"Did you notice the kids lying on their tummies on the oversized pillows? I'm glad you thought of it," Melanie said.

Lila stifled a giggle. "They are precious." She glanced at her watch. "Well, I'd better get moving. It's show time."

Melanie gave her a light pat on the back. "Good luck, Lila. Not that you need it. You're already a rock star in my eyes and someone else's." Lila followed her gaze toward Conrad. "He's watching you," she sang.

Lila waved a hand. "You're beginning to sound like Aunt Cathy," she warned with a waggling finger and walked to the front of the room to welcome the audience.

She was halfway through her second reading when her eyes caught Conrad's. With a quick wink, he filled her with a confidence she didn't realize was missing. She fought the rush of a school girl about to be kissed and struggled to strengthen the weak hold she maintained on her emotions.

An hour later, Lila invited the crowd to stay and mingle and enjoy the food and beverages. With a tray of scones in her hands, she made her way toward Conrad and his mother but was interrupted by a tug-tug-tug on her skirt. A set of beautiful triplets, of Asian descent, peered up at her. Lila guessed they were about ten-years-old.

She handed the platter of scones to Conrad. "Do you mind holding this for me?"

He accepted the platter from her without asking why. "Not at all—I'm not as pretty as you are, but would you like me to work the room, too?"

"If you don't mind," she answered. She bent down, eye level with the girls.

"Well, how absolutely adorable you three are tonight. Thank you for coming to my book signing. Are those new dresses you're wearing?"

Three heads nodded up and down, as precious as baby chicks in a hen house, their smiles as fresh as the county's first picking of sweet corn.

"Would you like to ask me something?"

One of the little girls with pink ribbons in her hair stepped forward after gentle prodding from the other two. "Can you write a book for us?"

Lila tilted her head. If she'd received a compliment as kind as this one in the recent past, she couldn't remember it. "Well, what kinds of stories do you girls like to read?" She had to give this some thought. Having no children of her own, Lila had no idea what little girls read. "Adventure?" she asked remembering the hype over the Harry Potter series.

Their eyes widened, but their body language told Lila to try again.

"OK," Lila tapped a finger against her cheek as if in deep thought. "How about mystery?"

"Oh, yes, and spooky too," the little spokesperson for the group said. It appeared to Lila she was using all the courage she had in order to ask the question.

Bingo she hit the jackpot. This could be the very inspiration she was looking for, but it would mean leaving the world of women's fiction, a place she was comfortable in and had been for the last decade. Lila retrieved three small writing tablets with pencils from her pocket, each one tied with a raffia string bow. She'd found them in the stationery section of the store. "Now, I have something to ask of you." She placed a writing tablet in each of their hands. "I'd like you to write down some spooky ideas for me and place them in the big owl jar on the counter. Is that a deal?"

"Deal. Deal. Deal." The three little angels sang. "Thank you, Miss Lila."

"You're welcome. Now off you go back to your parents." When she rose, Conrad handed her the platter of scones. "So, I'm not the only one with a soft spot for kids, am I?"

Lila accepted the scone tray back from him. "Weren't they adorable? Who could resist such innocence?"

Conrad arched a brow. "Are you going to do it?"

Lila stared at the face of the man she'd never grow tired of. "Hmm? Do what?"

Conrad bent his head keeping their conversation between them. "Write a children's book?"

"I might. Wouldn't that be a refreshing change?"

"It certainly would. I've been eyeing your scones. I

think I'm going to take the challenge and try one." He licked his full lips. "Any warning before I do?" His hand hovered over one of the largest scones on the platter, yet he waited for the go-ahead.

If they were alone, Lila wouldn't hesitate to punch him in the arm. Instead, she bounced a smile right back at him. "Fear not, I was supervised through every step. I must admit, they do look delicious, don't they?"

"I thought you weren't supposed to judge a book by its cover?"

"Go ahead and take one or I'll do it for you."

Conrad maneuvered the napkin over the platter. "OK, OK, Miss Pushy."

Lila offered Mrs. Hamilton a scone. "I'm so very happy you're here tonight. Did you enjoy the presentation?"

Mrs. Hamilton beamed in Lila's attention. "I loved it. I'm one of your biggest fans."

"Thank you. I hope I never disappoint."

Mrs. Hamilton smiled. "Lila, a thought occurred to me just now. We could really use your voice in the Christmas choir at church. You remember the director, Mr. Abbott. He's been running the show for over twenty years."

Lila nodded. "Of course, he was one of my favorites."

"We're going to start practicing on the first Monday in December. Even Conrad said he'd be interested in joining. So, there'd be another familiar face for you."

Conrad raised his hands. "Remember now, that's if my schedule allows it."

Mrs. Hamilton waved away her son's concern as if that was the least of her worries. "What do you say,

Lila? Will you join the choir and help us out?"

"I'm not sure about making a fulltime commitment. I'm due back in New York Christmas week, but I'm tempted to say yes. Thank you for inviting me." Lila loved the idea. Singing in the choir always ushered in the spirit of Christmas for her.

"We'll take whatever you're able to give us. And Conrad wouldn't mind giving you a lift. You may be asked to sing with the choir on Sunday mornings if Mr. Abbott needs you. Are you OK with that?"

Lila gave Conrad a quick side glance to find him shrugging his shoulders at his mother's suggestion as to say it was all good with him. "I'd love it."

"He'll be tickled to include your voice in the choir again. By the way, the scones are wonderful."

"Thank you. I helped Melanie bake them."

"You keep this up, and there'll be another baker in your family."

"Oh, I hope so, Mrs. Hamilton. Aunt Cathy would be so proud."

At the mention of her name, Lila's aunt joined them. "These scones are out of this world good. How are you, Mabel?"

Mrs. Hamilton laid a hand on her chest. "Impressed. It was a lovely event tonight. I really enjoyed Lila's ability to be so honest on stage."

Aunt Cathy flashed an 'I'm proud' smile, leaving little room for argument. "She doesn't hold back, does she?"

"I'm so thankful to Conrad for bringing me tonight. Not all children are as good to their parents."

Aunt Cathy took a seat next to Mrs. Hamilton. "I'm enjoying a blessing of my own with Lila back home again."

Lila almost missed the wink Mrs. Hamilton's gave Aunt Cathy. "Oh, indeed, and perfect timing if I may add."

"What do you mean?" Lila asked.

Mrs. Hamilton shifted in her seat. "Oh, for you to be a part of the Christmas choir, of course."

"Ahh, yes." Lila said.

Mrs. Hamilton was holding something back.

Lila would give it more thought later. The weight of Conrad's gaze was on her. "I honestly enjoyed your presentation. In fact, I'm considering reading one of your books. Which one would you recommend?" He sunk his teeth into the scone he was holding between his fingers.

"You do that, Mr. Hamilton, and I'll take up cooking. As long as I've known you, reading was never one of your favorite things to do."

Conrad finished the last bite of the scone and licked his fingers clean of the remaining icing. He hesitated a minute before he spoke again. "Well," he drawled out the word, "things change with time, don't they?"

Was he implying there was hope for them?

He rubbed a napkin across his mouth. "That was really good, by the way. I could go for another."

Lila's heart picked up a beat. She needed a miracle to make things right between them.

Lila followed Conrad's gaze to Melanie seated on a quilted stool behind the register. Jack stood at her side, bundling Lila's books with twine for the next customer.

"It's good watching Jack with Melanie. They've got a marriage that's envied by many people," Conrad said.

There wasn't much Lila could argue with that point.

"How did you manage to get Melanie to sit down?" Conrad tossed his napkin in the waste basket behind him.

"I signed all the books earlier today, and arranged them behind the counter so she and Jack would be able to chat with the customers during the checkout process. It helps establishing new relationships for further business down the road."

"Correct me if I'm wrong but it sounds like you're really getting the hang of running a small business."

"I must admit, I find it a refreshing break. I told Melanie I'd step in for her every afternoon starting tomorrow. Jack wants her home now that she's getting along in the pregnancy, and I'm available."

Conrad glanced at her. "Where does your writing fit in? Isn't that your top priority?"

"I can handle both. Once I get hold of an idea for my next book, it takes off."

"And you think you have an idea?"

"After my conversation with the triplets, yes."

He threw her a quizzical glance. "I'm not following how this all works."

Lila paused. "OK, close your eyes for a moment and picture a horse, a buggy, and a rider."

Conrad followed her instructions, but Lila wasn't prepared for her impulse to kiss his full lips.

"Ah, how long do you want me to stand around like this with my eyes closed?"

"Right, sorry. Try to imagine the horse as the characters in your story and the rider in the buggy as the writer. There are times the story takes off all on its own like a horse trotting down a road. The writer follows behind like the buggy rider. Every so often, the story needs a little guidance or a plotline—like a tug on the reins."

Conrad opened his eyes. "Sounds as if you need an organized mind to keep that all straight. Outside of that, it doesn't seem too hard."

Lila stared, open mouthed. She never expected that response from him. "Oh, is that right? You ought to give it a try sometime. And as far as being organized goes, I may be able to help you out with that. You seem to be running around like a chicken with your head cut off."

Conrad shook his head. "Oh, really? So now you're claiming to be able to run my business as well as Melanie's?"

"Oh, for goodness' sake, I'm only suggesting..." Lila turned from Conrad to find Cathy and Mrs. Hamilton wearing a couple of satisfied grins. How much of the exchange had they witnessed? Enough by the looks of them. They huddled together like two fat cats that managed to finish a generous bowl of milk.

Lila leaned toward Conrad. "I'd better get back to socializing with the other guests."

Conrad grinned. "If you have trouble pawning off the rest of the scones, I'll be happy to take them off your hands."

Lila rolled her eyes and turned away from him.

A woman, in a smart business suit and wearing high heels sashayed toward Lila.

"Suzanne," Lila swallowed back the surprise and kept her voice even.

"Well, isn't this like old times?" Suzanne entered the group, and the attention of those in the gathering, focused on one of the most beautiful women in Sister

Bay. Her sleek blonde hair tinted with the lightest of copper red highlights was tied in a Celtic knot at the nape of her neck, giving her flawless complexion no competition. High sculpted cheekbones glittered in soft peach, and she wore a little darker shade on her full lips. The icy coolness coming from Suzanne was undeniable, yet even Lila couldn't take her eyes off of her. If she didn't understand what drew Conrad to her before, she did now.

Aunt Cathy took a step back while Lila scanned the group. Conrad's face was tinged red, and his eyes were wide.

"What a nice surprise." Lila forced as much politeness into her voice as she could manage.

"Is it? What a turnout. I must admit I'm surprised." Suzanne's green eyes remained flat. Her intention cutting to the quick. Conrad stepped forward, his shoulder brushing Lila's, as if he were protecting her from the first blow in a battle. "I thought you were booked with a meeting tonight. You were more than welcome to come with Mom and me." He extended his hand, and Suzanne walked toward him as if accepting a dance request.

"That was this morning, darling. It's all right. I don't expect you to remember my schedule."

"How is business, Suzanne?" Aunt Cathy asked. "I suspect it's as slow for you as it is for every other shop in the village."

Much like the moment the Christmas tree at Rockefeller Center was plugged in for the first time of the holiday season, the shift in expression on Suzanne's face went from anger to joy. "That may be true for some, but our business is booming. With the new Ski Hill going in, there's more interest in second home purchases, which means more business for Hamilton Construction." Suzanne's eyes shifted at Conrad with an implied meaning for him and him alone.

Now Lila understood the alliance that acted like cement between Conrad and Suzanne. She was not only his intended, but she managed to wiggle her influence to financially help out Hamilton Construction, as well.

Mrs. Hamilton stifled a yawn. "Conrad, I think it's time."

"OK, Mom." Conrad turned a shoulder facing Suzanne. "I'm going to take Mom home. Where are you parked?"

Suzanne stepped into the small circle of people and laid a pretty manicured hand on Conrad's shoulder for support, kissing his left cheek. "Always the gentleman, Conrad. I'm a few blocks down the street."

Cathy rolled her eyes, and Lila exhaled. Was it the same relief filling Lila with the news Suzanne was leaving?

"Are you ready, Mom?" Conrad's words cut the air as thick as Lila's scone batter.

Mrs. Hamilton gave the group a courteous smile. "Good night, everyone."

"Good night and thank you again for coming," Lila said.

Suzanne's appearance had snuffed out the magic left in the evening and managed to take it right along with her. Lila's heart gave a tug as Conrad helped his mother slip on her coat. The best part of the signing was about to end.

"Good night, ladies." Conrad's eyes moved across the group delivering a quick wink of thanks at Lila.

Cathy shared a sleepy smile. "I'll watch for you on Sunday in church, Mabel. Always good to run into you, Conrad."

Conrad eased his mother through the crowd on their way to the checkout counter, his hand on her back as he navigated the room, Suzanne at his side. The effect of his absence from the room was immediate like a balloon gone flat. There was a chance she'd run into him tomorrow if he remembered she'd be working in the afternoon. She placed the scone platter on a nearby stand and looped her arm with Cathy's, grateful for the comfort of someone who loved her. Things were changing between her and Conrad. She could sense it, and she didn't need to ask.

Her aunt believed it, too.

14

When Lila arrived at the store the following day, she found Melanie behind the counter, seated on a stool. The lines around her eyes deeper than the night before.

"Well, I'm glad you're sitting down." Lila tried her best to sound upbeat.

Melanie rubbed her forehead. "Not much choice. My ankles are swollen to twice their size." She lifted her pant legs to reveal two puffy ankles.

"Ooh, that must hurt." Lila placed her purse and lunch bag under the counter.

Melanie groaned. "It's more of a throbbing pain and only when I'm on my feet too much. I think I overdid it last night, but I couldn't help myself. What a fantastic turnout. The sales made the whole difference."

"I'm glad, but that means today you take it easy. I'm here now. You tell me what needs to be done."

"We expect Conrad sometime today to disassemble the riser. Our job is to get the store back into shape. We can start by folding up the chairs. After that, it's Thanksgiving decorating time—my favorite time of the year."

Lila folded the chairs, starting with the back row, and placed them in the corner away from customers. She'd find out where Melanie wanted them placed when she had them all folded.

Conrad walked through the back door, bringing

with him a gust of wind. Dried, withered leaves followed his footsteps into the store. The warm weather they'd enjoyed over the weekend gave way to a late-night cold front with an early prediction of snow.

He wore an insulated jacket, one typical of men who worked in the outdoors. It added a layer of brute force to his already Herculean attractiveness. His dark curls peeked out from a black knit hat that bore the Sister Bay Bowl logo on the front, a reminder for Lila that he was taken. She folded the next chair in front of her and tried to keep her mind and body busy.

Conrad walked toward the front of the store. "I came down from Ellison Bay. It's already snowing up there. They're preparing for five-to-six inches of the stuff."

Melanie beamed a bright smile that breathed life into her face. "Oh, how wonderful. I want plenty so I can cuddle with my boys inside and watch the snowflakes fall."

"Mel, you're such a romantic." Lila clasped her hands together. "That does sounds lovely, so I'll agree with you but only if the snow comes in small doses."

Melanie smiled. "It would help the Ski Hill and the store to have a good snow year."

Conrad turned to Lila. "I wouldn't expect you to say you're looking forward to snow after remembering how afraid you are of the storms."

He remembered.

"Well I'm all grown up now and I love the winter months as much as summer. Most New Yorkers complain about it because of the inconvenience for them. Snow melters march in and it's soon gone and never enjoyed like we do here at home."

Conrad crossed the floor, closing the gap between

them. He brought with him the smell of freshly cut evergreen boughs. His cheeks were flushed. "Melanie's right. It will definitely add to the excitement for the new Ski Hill." He slipped off his coat and hat and walked toward the front of the store where the riser waited for him. "Melanie, I've scheduled a month for the ski chalet addition. Are we still moving forward?" he asked as he withdrew a screwdriver from his utility belt.

Melanie eased off the stool, walking on tentative feet. "I've got the permit and can picture it already—a big gas fireplace, oversized pillows on comfy extra-wide couches, a cozy gathering place. I'll make a point to go over the numbers again tonight."

"How did you ever think of the idea?" Lila asked.

Melanie's face colored with excitement. "When I found out the village wouldn't be building a lodge of its own, I seized the opportunity. I've been thinking about this for a long time. The sled riders and skiers will be seeking a warm place to congregate after a day on the hill to enjoy a hot chocolate and something to eat. You know my philosophy about feeding my customers."

Lila smiled. "It might lead to another sale."

"Right and a whole new stream of income."

"When does construction begin?" Lila was beginning to inherit some of Melanie's enthusiasm for the project.

"Our sales doubled since your arrival, and the signing last night pulled us out of the red. But finances are still tight. I may not be able to swing it this year."

"I have an idea. How about I pitch in and finance the addition?" Lila offered. She lifted her gaze to the corner of the room, weighing the impulsive suggestion, and nodded.

Melanie's mouth dropped open. "What do you mean?"

Lila's heart fluttered. "I can easily cover the cost, and I'd love the opportunity to help."

Melanie stared openly at her and appeared to be at a loss for words. "That's an extraordinary offer but I'm not sure when I could repay you."

Lila waved a hand. "We can work that out in the new year."

"If I were you, I'd grab it." Conrad shot a wink in Melanie's direction. "It's awfully generous of you, Lila." He placed one of the wood planks on the floor.

"I believe Melanie and the store are two solid investments. There's really nothing for me to even think about."

Melanie gazed down at the rug beneath her feet. It appeared she was giving Lila's suggestion serious consideration. She met Lila's gaze with moistened eyes. "I'm flabbergasted. All I can say is yes, yes. Yes! That would be fantastic, and the job is already on Conrad's schedule. The concrete was poured back in August."

Lila held her breath. Spending time with Conrad was not a good idea. Not for her. If only the world wasn't so right when she was near him. Goodness, he was about to propose to another woman!

How would she abandon her foolish thoughts of wanting more? She'd find a way to ignore him and her growing desire. She exhaled, almost resigning herself to the truth. Conrad was taken and wishing it could be different would get her nowhere.

Melanie walked toward Lila. "Conrad, let's move forward," she said. "All systems go."

He gave her a thumbs-up. "We'll get it done in time for the Ski Hill's grand opening. I've got a small job over in Bailey's Harbor for the next couple of weeks, but after that I'm all yours."

Conrad's words swirled in Lila's head. *I'm all yours.* How she wished that was true.

15

As the weeks in October faded away and November rolled in, Lila couldn't remember a time in her life so physically exhausting, nor could she recall loving it as much as she did.

She stole a peek at the calendar when she checked someone out at the store. If not for that, she'd have trouble believing so many weeks had passed. She'd reported to the store in the afternoons and worked until close. Each day, she tackled the milestones of small business management—from customer service to inventory maintenance to stocking the kitchen and baking scones. Melanie wanted her to have a level of confidence in running the store in case she needed her to step in.

In the evenings after supper, Lila started her new book and also began to chart out a children's mystery series she hoped to pitch to her agent. The little girls she'd met at the signing inspired her in a whole new direction. She only hoped Andrea and Jim would be as excited for that project as they would be for her next women's fiction story.

The pounding of nails announced Conrad's hard work. He'd been busy on the addition, trying to keep his promise to Melanie to have it done mid-December.

Melanie had decided to work the afternoon so she and Lila could finish inserting feathers into a five-foot-tall wooden turkey destined for the display window, their last task before closing.

Melanie let out a shriek. Her eyes rounded.

Lila spun in her direction. "What is it?"

Melanie leaned back, sucking in a deep breath.

"Conrad! Conrad, come quick!" Lila yelled.

Conrad ran toward them. "What is it?"

"Oh." Melanie inhaled and puffed breaths out a bit at a time.

Panic threatened to cut off Lila's air supply. "Something told me to send you home early today. Now I wished I would've listened. What should I do?" Without being told, Lila pulled a chair over to Melanie. "Let me help you sit down."

In the next moment, Conrad was next to them. He dropped to his knees at Melanie's side. His gaze swung from Melanie to Lila. He wanted answers, but all Lila could do was shake her head. This was so out of her experience.

"I was planning on going home, but I wanted to view the turkey in the window as if I were a customer." Melanie moaned.

Lila brushed Melanie's hair from her eyes. "It's going to be all right."

Conrad reached for his phone. "I'm calling Jack. Thank goodness he's sticking close to home these days."

Melanie sighed. "I think you'd better. Lila, can you call Dr. Hudson for me? My phone is in my purse under the counter. He's in my contacts list."

Lila bolted for the purse. Melanie warned her of complications as she neared her due date, but that was still six weeks down the road. Punching in the doctor's number, she handed the phone to Melanie. The electricity in the room hit an all-time high while Melanie spoke to her doctor, and Conrad paced the store waiting for Jack's arrival. Ten minutes later, Jack strode through the back door, his shoulders speckled with new-fallen snow. "I guess this means they were contractions, not Braxton Hicks?" he asked Melanie as if Lila and Conrad were not in the room.

Melanie gave her husband a half-hearted smile. "I think so. We're supposed to meet Doc Hudson at the hospital."

Conrad stepped forward. "What can we do?"

Melanie breathed her way through another wave of pain.

Jack took over. "Can you help me get her in the car? I'm parked right out back." Jack slipped Melanie's arms into her coat.

"On the count of three, we lift her." One, two, three and up Melanie went into the arms of the two men. Step-by-step, they walked together toward the back entrance.

"Easy does it now, honey. Everything's going to be all right," Jack murmured to his wife.

Lila sprung ahead and jogged up the exit ramp and held open the door. She shivered as a burst of wind and snow whipped across her face.

"I never thought I'd be the first one to need this ramp." Melanie puffed through the pains.

"You're always one step ahead," Jack said with obvious pride.

Lila watched as Jack and Conrad eased Melanie into the passenger side of the car. There was nothing more for her to do. Jack promised to call as soon as he knew more, and in the next moment, they were gone, the excitement over.

Conrad rushed back to the door Lila held open for him. "Wow!" he raked a hand through his thick hair.

The exhilaration on his face was contagious. They experienced something amazing. Together. Although Lila hoped she was wrong, it was very possible the twins were on their way into the world.

"Was that exciting or what?" He gripped her forearm in a gentle hold, drawing her close to him, an old habit he used often with her.

What passed between them next told Lila she needed to be careful. Their history was snowballing to the present, the chemistry they'd been fighting taking off like the bonfires they'd attended in their youth.

"Oh, you're not kidding. It makes me want a baby all the more. You, too?" Lila asked.

The weight of her words showed in his face. He released her. "That's not part of my future. It could be down the road, but it's a long shot. Suzanne's focus is on her career, not starting a family. It's part of the deal."

The same shadow of disappointment shrouded his face the last time they spoken of having children.

"Most women want children at some point in their life, and you seem to be skilled in the art of persuasion."

Conrad pursed his lips and shrugged. "She has no patience for children. That's not a good sign."

"Isn't that something you want to have nailed down before proposing?" Lila bit her bottom lip, wondering if she'd been presumptuous.

He lifted his shoulders in a light shrug as if it didn't matter, but children mattered to Conrad very much.

"You're probably right. Suzanne's motivated to succeed in everything she does. I get the impression that kids would get in her way. I've decided to let it go for now."

Why did he think letting a problem fester was the right move to make? The thought of Conrad giving up on being a father physically pained her. As premature as it had been, even they'd talked about kids, and she remembered his excitement at the prospect.

"What happens next with the store?" He changed the subject.

"Melanie's prepared me to take over in case of an emergency. It appears that time is now. Aunt Cathy is willing to come in and help if I need her. And Melanie's mother's flying in the week before Christmas. She'll take over at the store during Mel's maternity leave."

Conrad frowned. "Melanie's mother."

Lila tilted her head. "You sound surprised."

"Her mother worked here part-time for a while, but if I remember right, I don't think they got along really well. Melanie said they embodied different philosophies about running the place."

"That doesn't sound good." Had Melanie run out of viable options? Lila made a mental note to discuss it with her when things returned to normal. Lila turned over the "Closed" sign and locked the door.

"Closing up for the night?"

"It's time." She only wished she had a reason for them to stay. Instead, she snapped off the lights to the front of the store.

"You wouldn't be interested in picking up a burger, would you? Suzanne's working late tonight, and I really don't want a can of chunky soup again."

How could she say no to that request? She was famished, but the truth was, if anyone but Conrad had asked, she'd never consider it. "Are you kidding? I'd love a patty melt and onion rings."

Conrad grinned. "I thought so."

She turned to him, her face begging the question.

"You've got that 'I'm dying for a burger' look written all over you."

Lila let out a hearty laugh. "Oh, is that right? So now you're telling me you can read me like a book?"

He gave her one of his rare million-dollar smiles. "Always could."

"Aha. Let's go." She grabbed her coat and purse off the hooks in the office, and walked through the door he'd opened for her.

❄❄❄❄

When Lila stepped into Husby's Food & Spirits and took a quick glance at the menu, her eyes grew to the size of saucers. There were fourteen mouth-watering burger variations.

"This is an outstanding menu. I'm not sure what to order."

Conrad rubbed his chin. "I figured you'd like it. Why don't you get your favorite, the patty melt with onion rings?"

"Well, the onion rings are separate. They don't come with the burger, fries do."

"My treat tonight. Let's let her rip."

Lila giggled. She released the barrette that kept her hair presentable during the work day, but now with Conrad, she could relax and allow her hair the freedom it craved. She found his eyes upon her when she peered over the menu and wished she'd slathered a fresh coat of lipstick on her mouth before she'd taken a seat across from him.

A waitress approached their table, pencil in hand, ready to take their order.

Conrad handed the waitress the menus. "I'm going with the primetime burger with a slice of Colby."

Lila scanned the selections. "I'd like a patty melt."

The waitress straightened the checked apron around her waist. "Fries?"

Conrad bent over the table. "If you want the onion rings instead of the fries, order them."

Lila grinned. "I'd like to switch out the fries for the onion rings, please."

The waitress scribbled on her notepad. "It shouldn't be too long."

"Would you add two root beer floats to the order please?" Conrad asked.

Lila blinked hard. He remembered everything right down to their favorite drink.

The waitress stuck the pencil behind her ear. "You got it."

A woman meandered through the restaurant, waving in Lila's direction. "Is that…?"

Conrad turned to look. "Mrs. Albright, yes." He stood to greet the woman.

As a teenager, Mrs. Albright hired Lila often to babysit her children.

As she neared, Mrs. Albright's smile brightened the room. "Well, who do we have here? If it isn't Lila and Conrad. It is so good to run into you two young people again. How are you, Lila?"

Lila gave her a slow smile. "Thank you, Mrs. Albright, I'm well. Conrad and I are just—"

Mrs. Albright laid a light hand on the table. "You babysat our children years ago. You were so good to them. I also remember finding you, Mr. Hamilton, on my couch more often than once." She wiggled a wrinkled finger at Conrad.

Conrad raised both of his hands in surrender. "I promise you nothing inappropriate was going on."

Mrs. Albright's attention shifted from Conrad to Lila and back again. She released a laugh that sounded as delicate as a cardinal's song. "I noticed the stars in your eyes at that time, young man, as I do now. There's no fooling an old woman."

Lila cheeks burned.

The waitress placed their floats and on the table but was interrupted by a younger woman.

"Mother, there you are." Maggie, Mrs. Albright's oldest and a much younger version of the elderly woman approached the table with an apology written across her face. "I went to pay the bill and turned around, and she was gone. I'm so sorry. Oh, hello, Lila. Conrad."

"Actually, we were enjoying a wonderful conversation reminiscent of old times. Thank you for saying hello, Mrs. Albright." Lila said.

"They think because I'm old I'll run off with the postman and forget where I live," she whispered. "It was so pleasant to visit with you both." And with a wink to Lila, she left with her daughter.

Conrad worked the ice cream in his glass. "That was sweet."

"She has a pretty good memory despite her age. I hope I'm that lucky."

Conrad's smile deepened. "The Albrights celebrated their fiftieth anniversary not too long ago. Big article in the paper. You wonder how many couples will make it that far today."

Was he thinking of his own destiny with Suzanne?

Lila was about to ask the question when their food arrived. Conrad picked up his steak knife, cut his sandwich straight down the middle, and separated his fries into two piles. He pushed his plate toward the center of the table and smiled.

Lila pinched herself to make sure what she was witnessing was real. This had been their ritual whenever they went out for burgers. She'd thought he'd long since forgotten about it. With the expertise of a practiced sous chef, Conrad lifted one half of the sandwich off his plate. Lila followed his lead with her own sandwich. He slid his half on her plate, and she placed her half on his. They divided up the onion rings and French fries in the same way.

"Like old times," he said and took an enormous bite from his burger.

She raised her gaze to meet his. "The best memories of my life."

He squinted at her as if he may have misheard.

Lila reached for an onion ring, dunked it into a mound of ketchup, and lifted it to her mouth.

Her point hit home.

16

The Wednesday before Thanksgiving, Lila jotted down a list of the sold-out items for inventory purposes.

Conrad walked into the kitchen. He was instructing the workers to take their lunch break and she assumed he would do the same. He kept a tight rein on his subcontractors and usually broke for lunch when they did.

Lila had taken over for Melanie after the doctor had been able to stop her early labor and had ordered strict bedrest for his patient.

"How's the begruntled patient doing?" Conrad asked.

"She loves this store. It's been her life until now. How would you feel if you couldn't get up and do your job every day?"

"When you put it that way, I guess I can really feel for the girl." Conrad placed his metal lunchbox on the end of the island. He tilted his head. "I've got a sandwich inside of this little baby, but I could use some company. What are you doing there?" he asked, nodding toward her paperwork.

"I'm tallying the Thanksgiving sold-out items. We're completely out of all chocolate and paprika cloth napkins and the matching napkin rings and the brass-colored charger plates. If I suspected a run on those items, I would have ordered twice as many to hold us through the holiday."

"Sounds impressive. You keep track of that stuff, huh?" he asked as he flipped open his lunchbox.

"Well, yes, a simple inventory alerts you to what quantity to order for next year. Once I've got the tallies I'll input them into a spreadsheet."

"Hmm, sounds like a system that may work in my business."

"How do you mean?" Lila asked. She placed the pencil next to the paper and gave Conrad her undivided attention.

"In the spring of the year, we tend to do more deck and pergola construction. Summer's filled with additions and piers. Fall and winter projects move indoors—rec rooms, second bedrooms, or garage work. If I understood what caught me up the year before, I'd be able to better plan and avoid some of the fires I end up having to put out."

"I'd be happy to show you the spreadsheet program. It's the same one I use to organize my characters and scenes."

"Sounds good. I have to do something to keep things straight." He pulled out a peanut butter and jelly sandwich from his lunchbox.

"Don't tell me that's your lunch," Lila asked.

"It works in a pinch." He shrugged off her concern and acted as if he was holding a steak sandwich in his hand.

"At least allow me to heat up a bowl of the beef stew Aunt Cathy and I made the other day to go along with it. That's what I'm having."

"I'd like that. I don't make it over to Mom's enough to enjoy home cooking during the busy season."

"And Suzanne? Doesn't she cook?"

"Suzanne's as busy as I am and doesn't enjoy cooking. We eat out more than in."

Lila pulled out the quart container of soup and a few salad ingredients from the fridge. She placed them on the island. So, Melanie was right again. Suzanne didn't cook, either. Lila was beginning to wonder if she'd make a good wife for Conrad. She poured the soup into a stainless-steel pot, clicked the gas burner on low, and then reached for the lettuce to chop.

The bells over the entrance in the other room signaled the arrival of a customer. She dropped the knife. The handle hit the carton of cherry tomatoes at an angle, sending little red balls in all directions. "Oh, good grief!"

Conrad stood. "Don't worry about this. I'll take care of it."

"Thanks a million, Conrad. Sometimes I'm such a klutz in the kitchen."

She darted to the checkout counter to find three attractive women meandering through the store.

"Hello, ladies. How are you today?"

"Miranda, why don't you ask her for the item?" a tall pretty brunette suggested.

"We're searching for a Pipka Santa Claus," the woman asked.

The hair on the back of Lila's neck stood up. Something was off. "The local retailers don't carry them. However, you can find them at Pipka's. The store is a few blocks from here, right down on Mill Road. Are you visitors to Sister Bay?"

"No, we're local," Miranda said.

If they were local, that much was common knowledge. Everyone in the village knew where to find Pipka's. The store was recognized worldwide.

One of the other women held up a hand-fired platter embellished with a Norman Rockwell Christmas scene, part of a six-serving set. "Oh, Jess, that is lovely."

"How much do you want for this?" Jess asked. She held the platter in one hand and lifted it slightly in the air.

Lila moved forward and gently took the piece from her. "I'm sorry, but this platter is part of a Christmas set. It's not available as a single item." Lila gestured to the matching plates, cups, saucers, and bowls on a nearby table. "The entire collection is priced at two hundred and fifty dollars."

Jess placed her hand on her chest. "What?" she asked as if the price shocked her right out of her high-heeled designer boots. "I'd like to talk with Melanie about that. Is she here?"

Lila returned the platter to its display holder. "Melanie is on medical leave. I'm in charge of the store until her return."

The other woman stepped toward Lila. She tucked her red leather clutch under her arm as if she'd need both of her hands free. "And who are you?" she asked with a tilt of her head. Cat-like eyes, outlined in kohl eyeliner, glared at Lila for an immediate answer.

Lila took an intake of breath to diffuse her nerves until the footsteps behind her drew closer.

"Hello, ladies," Conrad's tone implied that he'd caught three little girls with their hands in a cookie jar.

"Conny, hi," three voices harmonized a reply. "We didn't think you'd be here of all places today," Miranda gushed.

"Brittany." Conrad nodded toward the only one in the group whose name was unknown to Lila.

Brittany retraced her steps and aligned herself shoulder-to-shoulder with Jess.

"We thought we'd stop in over our lunch break," Miranda sputtered as if offering a peace treaty.

Jess gazed down at her oversized watch. "But we really should be getting back. It's almost time." She tapped a red-painted fingernail against the watch's face.

Brittany nodded. "Yes, I think you're right. Thank you for your help ah—"

"Lila," Conrad advised.

"Yes, thank you, Lila, and please give Melanie our kind regards."

Lila was relieved to watch the trio leave. "Thank you for stopping in, ladies. I'll be running a nice sale on Black Friday. Do come back and visit us again."

After they left, Lila turned toward Conrad and released a breath. "Friends of yours?"

He shook his head. "Not mine. Suzanne's."

His tone told Lila the three women never would be friends of his either. "Ah, that makes sense. Come on, you. Let's get back to that lunch of ours."

"Sounds good to me."

They were becoming a team. Lila smiled. If only it could last forever.

❄❄❄❄

With everything going on, Thanksgiving came and went with little notice. Lila and Conrad wished each other a nice day, but the realization that they couldn't spend the holiday together didn't sit well with Lila. Conrad told her that he and Suzanne were invited over to Luke's house this year, but Suzanne's preference was to accept her parents' invitation in order to enjoy the day in peace without having to tend to Luke's children. Not wanting another argument, Conrad agreed.

Lila and Cathy spent the morning watching the parade on TV and enjoying a roasted duck. They played Scrabble and then took a leisurely walk around the neighborhood. As far as Lila was concerned, it was one of the best Thanksgivings she'd enjoyed in a long time. It certainly beat her typical routine of picking up a premade turkey dinner from one of the gourmet grocers and dining alone while watching a Christmas movie.

A few days later Lila wandered through the store while on her usual mid-day call with Melanie.

A cold draft swirled around Lila as she approached the store's front entrance. "*Brr.* I think it's time to switch out the screen door for the winter storm door," Lila explained.

"Oh, sure, it's in the back of the large closet in the kitchen. Why don't you ask Conrad to come over and do it?"

"Because he's a busy man. I found the hammer last week and pounded down all the loose floorboard nails. I think I can tackle this little job."

"My, oh my. Aren't we becoming handy?"

Lila giggled at the thought—her handy with tools? "You don't realize what you can do until you try."

"You sound pretty confident. How about you pushing these two babies out for me?"

"Oh, no. You got yourself in that pickle."

"I hope to be saying the same back at you one day. How's the chalet addition going?"

"He's working hard to get it finished on time.

Then all the room will need is a good coat of paint and for the furniture to arrive."

"Well, he'll make sure the contractors show up and the furniture is delivered. That's what I love about Conrad. He told us he'd finish by mid-December and he'll come through."

Lila wanted to agree but with a whole different set of reasons for loving Conrad. "Yes, he's a man of his word."

"I read in the newspaper that everything's in place for the Ski Hill's grand opening. I hope I was right to go ahead with this addition. What do you think now that it's nearing completion?"

"Let me ask you something—was there ever a time that you've been wrong about anything involving the store?"

"Ah…yes, but I tend to bury those little incidents."

"My advice is to continue to believe in your instinctual ability to run a business. It usually guides you in the right direction, and it will come through for you again."

❄❄❄❄

When the calendar turned over to the first days in December, icy winds and frequent snow showers arrived. The outermost edges of the lake froze over and the native birds became scarce. Tourism slowed, and so did the local customers. It wouldn't be long and the cross-country skiers and snowmobilers would bring new life back into the village, but until that happened, Lila grew concerned with each passing day. She needed a spark to draw attention to the store so they wouldn't lose the upward momentum they gained since her arrival.

"What do you do to bring in customers this time of year?" Lila worked in the kitchen and talked on the phone with Melanie.

"The Chamber had mentioned something about Santa Claus visiting the village this year. I wanted to arrange for him to come in for an hour or so in the afternoons and offer picture packages for our customers."

"I like the idea, and it's never too early for Santa. Who should I talk to arrange it?" Lila asked.

"Conrad may have some information. His uncle from Fish Creek has played Santa in the past."

Lila pulled in a slow breath. If he was about to propose to Suzanne, she'd better keep her distance. He deserved every right to happiness. She was beginning to regret agreeing to sing in the Christmas choir. He'd reminded Lila that his mother had promised he'd give her a ride to practice, and she'd agreed without thinking it through. That was going to complicate matters.

"Or you could go to the chamber meeting in my place," Melanie interrupted Lila's thoughts. "It's held the first Wednesday of every month at Town Hall."

"That sounds better. That would be next Wednesday, right?"

"Yes. The director's name is Anne Richards. Introduce yourself and explain you're filling in for me. The Santa issue may already be on the agenda. If not, are you comfortable bringing it up?"

"Sure, that sounds easy enough."

"How's everything else going?"

"Are you asking about my writing and the fifty pages I need to have done?"

"Yes, that and…"

"Oh, you mean Conrad? I'm trying to keep my distance from him."

"I gathered that much. The question is why."

Lila glanced at the wood-planked floor, searching for the right words. "Because he's going to ask Suzanne to marry him this Christmas. That's plenty reason in my mind."

"Yes, unless something or someone prevents him from doing that. It's pretty obvious to me that whatever you and Conrad had in the past has reignited. There's a very special bond between you, and I'm not the only one who noticed the electricity the night of the signing."

Lila giggled and released the tension building inside of her with the subject of Conrad. "You're starting to sound like my aunt."

"And probably for good reason. Promise me you'll think about this and don't wait until it's too late."

Lila frowned. "Too late for what?"

"To tell him you've fallen back in love with him."

"It isn't fair to him if I…"

"When are you going to forgive yourself for a decision you made so many years ago?"

The weight of her consequences hit Lila hard as if she wore a backpack full of her own books. "I don't believe its right to interfere now, Mel."

"I want you to do something for me. Follow your heart, not your head."

Did Melanie make a good point? "Did I tell you he's picking me up tomorrow night for choir practice?"

"What? How did this come about?" Melanie's surprise matched Lila's excitement.

Lila visualized the smile on Melanie's face.

"The night of the book signing, his mother asked me to join the choir and in the next breath she offered Conrad to pick me up on his way. Apparently, he's in the choir too."

Melanie let out a whoop. "Now we're talking. I remember you both used to sing in the choir."

Lila rubbed her hand across her forehead. "I hope I can still carry a tune."

Melanie giggled. "It's like riding a bike, I'm sure you'll do fine."

"Maybe you're right. I'm excited about going. I've missed singing and being in church."

Melanie stifled a yawn. "Sounds good, I think I'll take my afternoon nap now. Let's talk later."

Lila sighed with relief. Talking with Melanie always seemed to put her back on the right track. "Sweet dreams, my friend."

"And Lila?"

"Yes."

"Give your heart a break and a little room to breathe. Please?"

Lila's shoulders relaxed. What could it hurt? "OK."

17

Lila scanned her room at the mess she'd created. Her bed was littered with skirts, slacks, and sweaters. A few dresses hung on hangers over a doorknob.

"This will do," she muttered, referring to the dark blue pants and matching sweater she'd purchased from On Deck last month. "You'd think I was going to a special event of some kind, not a church choir practice." But this was no ordinary night. Conrad was picking her up and that made it anything but regular.

Lila snapped off the lights to her room, closed the door, and went downstairs in search of Aunt Cathy. Her aunt smiled when Lila walked into the kitchen and handed Lila a mug of hot coffee, a ritual they shared in the evening and one Lila enjoyed.

"Well, don't you look nice? Is that new?" Aunt Cathy stirred a sugar cube in her coffee.

Lila wrapped her hands around the warm mug. "It sure is. It's from On Deck." She inhaled the aroma of hazelnut as she brought the mug to her lips.

"Shopping local now, are you?" she asked with a raised eyebrow.

Lila smiled, "I guess I am."

"Sorry I can't join you and Conrad at choir practice tonight. Early this afternoon I noticed the aches and pains settling in. No fun getting old." She swept an arm across her body to accentuate her point.

"Oh, don't worry about that, it's the first night of practice. I'll explain it to Mr. Abbott. It's important you get well."

Funny, her aunt didn't appear unwell, but sometimes those things were hard to read. Lila repeated her aunt's words in her head—*you and Conrad*. It almost sounded as if they were a couple again.

"I hope you didn't feel like you were put on the spot to join the choir. I swear, every year Mabel Hamilton manages to rein in some of the best voices in Sister Bay, and she outdoes herself every time."

"I thought it was sweet of her to ask and to remember that I used to sing. I can't tell you how long it's been since I sang a hymn or went to church, for that matter."

"It's ironic the way things work out, don't you agree?"

Lila furrowed her brow. "What do you mean?"

"You and Conrad in the choir again. It's like old times." A Cheshire cat grin flashed across her face.

"I think the situation is more coincidental than ironic."

"Really?" Aunt Cathy sipped from her mug, appearing unimpressed with Lila's argument.

"Yes. You told me yourself Mrs. Hamilton is the director's right hand, and Conrad used to sing in the choir. You're not going to let your imagination run away with this, are you?"

Cathy pulled out a chair from the table and took a seat. "Why don't you tell me what you think is going on between you and Conrad? According to some folks, sparks are flying, and tongues are wagging. In a village this size, people take notice of that sort of thing and start yapping about it like they do when they're watching a new series on television."

"Oh, for goodness' sake, I'd forgotten how the smallest of details explode into a story here."

A heavy dose of guilt wiggled its way up Lila's throat. She assumed she'd been successful at disguising her attraction for Conrad, but apparently, she hadn't done so well. She must be more careful from now on. "Conrad and I are friends. We're simply getting reacquainted. It's mere coincidence that we were once in the Christmas choir and find ourselves there again."

"And the meal at Husby's?"

Lila opened her mouth to speak but thought better of it. Her aunt knew about Husby's?

Aunt Cathy smiled and waved her hands in surrender. "I want you to be aware of how things appear from another perspective, that's all. As far as I'm concerned, I love what's transpired between you two. You're meant to be together, and the sooner you both admit it, the happier you'll be."

"Even though he's about to walk down the aisle with someone else?"

"There's a reason why he's not engaged yet, Lila."

Lila breathed a sigh of relief when the doorbell chime sang out its melody, interrupting their conversation. That was until she stepped aside to let Conrad enter the room. He brought with him a scent of musk, cheeseburgers, and the outdoors. An attractive elixir for Lila. He wore a pair of new black jeans, a red Henley shirt, and an insulated winter white jacket and resembled a lumberjack and ski instructor rolled into one. His jacket crinkled as he rubbed his palms together. He flashed Lila a smile that weakened her knees. Goodness what this man did to her insides.

"Ladies, it's getting cold out there." His voice was

as smooth as a commentator on the local news.

Aunt Cathy's gaze jumped from Conrad to Lila and back to Conrad again. She walked over to the window and made herself comfortable in her favorite chair. "That's December in Door County. Before you realize it, Christmas will be upon us."

The adorable look of a boy on Christmas morning swept across Conrad's face. "And the reason I'm here. Are you ladies ready? I left the truck running so you'd be warm."

Aunt Cathy grabbed for a blue afghan and placed it on her lap. "I'm afraid I won't be going. I'm a little under the weather. You go on ahead with Lila."

Was it Lila's imagination or did Conrad conceal a smile? Whatever it was caused her heart to stop dead and a lump the size of Mt. Everest to form in her throat.

"I'm sorry to hear that Mrs. Williams. I hope it's not the flu. A lot's going around."

"Oh, don't you fuss about me. I'm as tough as they come, but a bit worn out. You two enjoy the evening and don't let Mr. Abbott ruin the night for you." She placed the hand-crocheted blanket across her lap.

"We'll do our best, won't we, Lila?" The words slipped off his tongue as if her aunt wasn't it the room, leaving Lila's mouth as dry as parchment paper. Lila couldn't tell if he was flirting with her or being kind. She offered him a weak smile and swallowed down her suspicions like a bitter pill. She must be misreading him. Sometimes her creative mind clashed with reality.

"Good night, you two," Aunt Cathy sang out from her chair.

"Good night," Lila and Conrad chimed together.

Lila ignored the guilt whispering in her ear for

heading out the door with another woman's almost-fiancé. Was Cathy right when she said he wasn't engaged yet for a reason? She remembered Melanie's advice to enjoy the moment. She met her aunt's gaze before closing the door and found an I-told-you-so smile waiting for her.

All Lila could do was return a smile which told her aunt that Lila knew she wasn't really ill. Then she joined Conrad, walking by his side toward his truck.

He opened the passenger-side door for her. Lila slid onto the warmed leather seat, appreciative that he left the truck running. The cab was as cozy as sitting in front of a roaring fire.

"Suzanne won't mind you giving me a lift to choir practice, will she?" She asked once he was settled inside.

Conrad shook his head. "Not really. We don't keep tabs on each other's every move. The last place she'd want me to take her is to church."

"What do you do together? If you don't mind me asking."

Conrad shrugged. "We used to bowl, but that's not really me. I did it—"

"To forget about me?"

"S'pose you're right about that."

"Did it work?"

Conrad exhaled. "I ended up dating Suzanne, so I guess it did. You said you came close to having some serious relationships too, didn't you?"

Lila released a disappointing sigh, "I did, but my aunt claims I picked the wrong men on purpose."

Conrad chuckled under his breath. "Is that possible?"

"I never thought about it until she brought it to my

attention. I'm not sure, but all the relationships ended one way or another."

"Why?" Conrad asked as he pulled up alongside the curb in front of their childhood church.

Lila shrugged as she opened her door. "I suspect I was comparing them to an impossible standard." She didn't expect Conrad to answer, and he didn't disappoint. Lila walked silently beside him on the sidewalk, buried in her thoughts.

Once inside, Lila stood next to Conrad in the back of the building. Her shoulders and neck relaxed in the familiar peace and quiet of her childhood church. The same life-sized statues of Joseph and Mary stood next to one another, gazing down at the infant Jesus. Six pillar candles cast a liquid gold blanket of light into the front of the sanctuary. It reminded Lila of the story declaring the illumination present over the manger in Bethlehem the night Jesus was born. She leaned in toward Conrad. "Can we sit down for a minute?"

"It appears we're the first ones here." He led her to one of the back pews and stepped aside, allowing her to enter first, the same gesture he'd always offered when they had dated.

Lila bowed her head and reflected on the last few years of her life. The time she'd spent in New York fooled her into the notion she didn't need her faith. Seduced by money, fame, and notoriety, she made the climb to the mountaintop without so much of a backward glance. What a fool she'd been. She'd lost the very essence of what gave life meaning—love.

She raised her eyes to the cross and wiped away the tears that collected in the corners of her eyes before Conrad noticed. She didn't deserve the forgiveness she prayed for because she'd hurt the one person who trusted her. He'd encouraged and supported her to follow her dreams but believed she'd come back to him.

He rested a warm hand on her knee, giving a reassuring squeeze. She dropped her gaze, wanting to reach out and place her hand over his. Did he understand her struggle, her regrets? A voice inside her told her to beg his forgiveness and tell him the truth—that she'd fallen back in love with him.

In the next blink of her eye, the church entrance lit up like the lights on a Christmas tree. Chatter and hushed laughter from the back of the church chased off the silence, which had been so pervasive a moment ago. In one synchronized movement, Lila and Conrad turned and looked over their shoulders to determine what the commotion was all about.

"Hello, hello, everyone, let's get started." Mr. Abbott sang out his greeting as he strolled down the center aisle of the church, his woolen coat draped over his left arm. He was holding sheet music in his hand. At least a dozen choir members followed behind him as if he were the Pied Piper. He stopped with a start at Lila and Conrad's pew, his eyes fixed on Lila.

"Oh, who do we have here? Lila Clark? And who do I have to thank for your participation tonight? I was expecting Mrs. Williams."

Lila stood to address her former choir director. "Mrs. Hamilton invited me to join the Christmas choir. She said you could use a few more voices and, unfortunately, my aunt is unwell this evening."

Mr. Abbott brushed a slender finger across his chin and smiled. "We certainly would not turn down a strong soprano voice such as yours, Ms. Clark. You are welcome to join us." He turned his gaze to Conrad.

"Mr. Hamilton. We can always use more tenors. Come along, you two. There's no time to spare."

Conrad shot Lila a devilish grin as they followed the group to the front of the church. She brushed up against his shoulder, closing the space between them. "What are you snickering about?"

"I think he remembers the prank we pulled on him years ago."

Lila had no idea what he was talking about.

"At one of our last choir practices."

Lila giggled.

People turned to look at them.

"I don't remember. What happened?" she asked.

"We loosened his music stand. As soon as he touched it, the whole thing fell down with such a force"—Conrad muffled his laugh behind the back of his hand—"The man jumped at least ten feet into the air."

Lila bit her bottom lip to avoid drawing attention. The last thing she wanted to do was make a fool of herself in front of the Christmas choir and Mr. Abbott. She couldn't believe Conrad remembered the prank.

"I wasn't part of that. You and the other tenors pulled that stunt."

Conrad winked. "Didn't I tell you all about it before it happened?"

"Ah..."

"You were an accomplice." Before she could utter another word in her defense, he jogged up the riser steps headed toward his section of the choir.

"Ms. Clark?" Mr. Abbott twirled around on the balls of his feet to face her. "If you would join the other sopranos who are ever-so-patiently waiting for you, we can get started this evening." His patience appeared to be wearing as thin as his hairline.

The heat in Lila's cheeks signaled her embarrassment. Like a schoolgirl being reprimanded for talking in the halls after the bell rang, she wiped the smile off her face and scrambled to take her place in the choir. If only Melanie could be here. For the first time in forever, she was happy to be right where she was, enjoying the moment.

18

Lila hadn't sung so much in years. A few minutes past nine o'clock Mr. Abbott thanked everyone for their hard work. "We'll meet next week, same time and place. Good night, all, and remember to protect those voices. I need each and every one of them."

Conrad approached. Lila told her fellow sopranos she'd be there next week.

He held her coat open, and she easily slipped inside. They walked out of the church following the others, making conversation, and in step with each other back to his truck. Their coats brushed up against one another, and Lila fought the urge to slip her hand into his.

Conrad cleared his throat. "That wasn't as bad as I thought. I had fun."

Lila tilted her head back toward the sky, maneuvering to catch the falling snowflakes in her mouth. "I loved it. It was like old times. It's been way too long."

When they reached the truck, he paused watching her. "You still think you're pretty good at catching snowflakes like that, don't you?" He opened the passenger-side door open for her.

"As a matter of fact, I do. Is there anything wrong with that?"

He raised his hands as if to surrender, a wide grin spreading across his face. "Not a thing. It's been a long time since I've seen anyone do it."

She slid into the seat but peered deep into the eyes that captivated her. "Since I've been home, I've realized there are a lot of things I've missed and haven't done in a long time." She closed the door before he responded.

Once he was behind the wheel, Conrad turned the key and fired up the engine.

Lila shivered. The cold seat fabric was successful, working a chill right up her spine.

Conrad pressed the heat button and flipped the seat warmers on high. A blast of cool air chased by hot blasted their faces.

"Ah!" Lila almost jumped off her seat.

Conrad adjusted the air vents and slid the levers to medium. "Sorry, I wanted to warm it up in here."

Lila thought him adorable for his concern for her. "It's OK. It did get cold."

He slipped the truck into drive. "So, you were about to tell me what other stuff you haven't done for a while."

Lila exhaled. Would Conrad ever understand the choice she'd made? "Singing was something I left behind in Sister Bay. That and going to church. When I think back, it's as if I said good-bye to the person I was in order to become who I thought I needed to be. Does that make sense?"

"It does. In a way, I've done the same thing."

She looked at him as if through a new lens. "How do you mean?"

"The not-going-to-church part at least. I guess I could blame it on Suzanne. She wasn't raised in the church, but I won't do that. I stopped going for no reason at all."

So, Conrad fell away from the church too. "It takes

a lot of courage to recognize our weaknesses, doesn't it?"

Conrad gave her a smile, "How does it feel slipping back into your old life?"

Lila sighed. "Like I've run into someone I haven't seen in a very long time."

"Wow. That's funny." Conrad tightened his grip on the steering wheel.

Lila shifted her gaze from the road to Conrad. "What?"

"I've been going through the same experience ever since you came back. In a way, it's as if I've found that pair of slippers I thought I'd lost."

Lila smacked his arm. She might as well of hit a block of ice. "Are you saying I'm a pair of old slippers?"

Conrad lifted his hand in defense. "Hey, don't take it the wrong way. I'm just trying to relate, that's all." He leaned with the vehicle as it curved around a bend in the road. "You like living in New York? I can't seem to picture you there, not the girl I used to date."

Lila wanted to ask him if he meant the girl he once loved. She sighed and chose her words with care. "New York is one of those crazy cities where the flight or fight instinct kicks in right away. It can energize you, making dreams come true, but if you let it, it has the power to drain you at the same time, robbing you of the very things that are important in life."

He stared straight ahead, driving at a steady pace toward Aunt Cathy's. "Sounds like you gave up a lot," he said.

"I did," she said, resignation in her voice. "It was the little things at first—running, raking leaves, shoveling the sidewalk. Or spending time outdoors doing nothing at all. New York is energizing but noisy, busy with busses, cabs, and airliners. Then there's Central Park, well, it's lovely but a hassle to get down to."

Conrad applied the brakes for a stop sign. "My company keeps me hopping all day long, but at least I can get outside and breathe the air, and it won't kill me. I can't say I envy you there."

"You're very blessed in that way. I spend a good part of the year behind a computer in a land of make-believe. The remaining months are spent on book tours, so I'm not able to be outside, much less connecting with nature. Being home again reminds me of what's important in my life."

"You used to love the outdoors, Lila."

"You're right, and please don't get the wrong impression of New York. It has a lot to offer: the theater, restaurants, and a night life that doesn't quit, if you're into that."

Conrad let out a long-drawn whistle. "I don't think I could live there. I'm used to working with my hands and being outside in the dirt, digging up night crawlers and fishing for bluegills. I guess, in a way, I've never grown up. It's a pretty simple way of life, but it works for me."

"I wouldn't downplay your life. You can drive around Door County, and the result of your hard work is right there in front of you. That's an accomplishment to be proud of."

Conrad huffed. "You're something, too. I'd lost track of how many books you've written until the night of the signing when all ten of them were staring me in the face. You made all your dreams come true."

Not all of them. Was now the time to tell Conrad

she wasn't sure it was worth it? "Let me ask you something. Do you think the paths we took were the ones we were meant to take?"

He shrugged. "That's a hard question to answer, and one I don't like thinking about much. How are you handling being away from New York? Miss it?"

"No." The word slipped off her tongue so fast it made his eyes leave the road for a moment to search hers.

"I'm struggling with burnout. I needed this time to recharge."

"Has it helped? Did you come up with a new idea for your next book?"

"Yeah. I think so, but it's going to be very different from anything I've written before." Lila slipped her bottom lip between her teeth. "To be honest, I don't know how my agent's going to take the news."

Lila's smartphone sang out its incoming-call signal, interrupting the conversation.

Conrad whispered. "Go ahead and take it. I'm in no rush."

Andrea's face lit up the screen. "It's Andrea."

Conrad gave her a quizzical glance. "Andrea?"

"My agent."

Conrad turned the corner and pulled up alongside Cathy's. "I hope that's a good thing." He slid the gear into park.

Andrea's voice was as crisp as the first cold winter day in Door County. "Lila, I've got some bad news. Jim has left the agency."

"We lost Jim?"

"He left Stonewood for good. They tried negotiating to keep him, but he'd been wanting out for quite a while. I was afraid this might happen. So, there's a decision you need to make. He's offered to take us with him to his new publishing house."

"What's the name of the company?" Lila asked.

"New Avenue Press."

Lila paused, trying to place the company. "I can't say I've come across their name."

"They're a little smaller and brand-new to the publishing scene. There is another option. We could try and pitch your next project to the new editor at Stonewood."

Lila waffled between relief and sadness. A season of her life was changing.

"Please tell me you've come up with some ideas for your next book."

"I have and I'm pretty excited to share them with you, but this is not a good time. I'm with Conrad right now."

"Who's Conrad?"

Lila hesitated and shifted her attention to Conrad. "Someone important."

"Oh, oh, Lila. Is everything OK out there?"

"Everything's fine. We'll talk soon and thanks for letting me know about Jim. Good night, Andrea."

"Well, it's my job and I care about what happens to you, Lila. Can't wait to hear about Conrad. Talk later."

After the call, Lila noticed the concern on Conrad's face.

"It's OK," Lila laid a hand on his arm. "Jim, my editor left my publisher, and my agent's a little agitated."

"That actually doesn't seem like the best of news."

"It's a change, that's all. I have a decision to make between moving with Jim to the new publishing house and taking a chance on a new editor at Stonewood."

Conrad shrugged. "What will you do?"

Her coat crinkled as she shrugged her shoulders. "I'm not sure. If Jim likes my idea for my next book, moving with him to the new publishing house makes sense, but if he doesn't, odds are the new editor will want me to keep writing the same material and stay put."

"Sounds like you're ready for something new."

"I think you're right." Lila cast her gaze down at her lap, the soft, rhythmic breathing of the man next to her giving her comfort. "Listen, I want to th—"

Before she could get the words out, Conrad's fingers lifted her chin.

His lips brushed over hers with the lightest of pressure before he kissed her deeply. Time stopped. She placed a hand on the side of his face. The years they were apart, vanished. A roller-coaster energy roared through her. No longer the writer in charge or the woman running Window Shopping, she was Conrad's girl again.

When they broke apart, she caught her breath, wishing she could stay in his arms forever. Her mind played catchup to her body's responses. She'd fallen back in love with him. Ooh, it was such a long time since she'd been kissed like that—years too long.

"Good night, Lila." His eyes softened in the corners along with his smile. "Are you coming to the chamber meeting on Wednesday in Melanie's stead? She makes it a practice to attend."

Lila scrambled to resettle her emotions, as if she were shelving the new inventory at the store. "Conrad, I…"

He laid a thick finger on her lips. "Before you say

anything, can we wait and enjoy what's happening here between us?"

"I like the sound of that, but what about Suzanne?"

"I've got some things to figure out, but I can't ignore this. Can you?"

Lila fiddled with the zipper on her coat. "No. But you need to be certain of your next steps of that much I'm sure."

He shifted in his seat, face relaxed, confident, and utterly appealing. "I'm not about to ignore what's going on with you and me, and I sense you don't want to either."

"I never expected to cause problems by coming home."

"Whatever happens, your returning into my life may have forced my eyes open. Ever thought of that?"

Lila pressed her lips together to fight a smile. "No?" she asked, her question delivered with a hint of surprise.

"Yes," he said in a tone that meant business. "I'll watch for you tomorrow night at the meeting."

She gathered up her things and gave him a twinkle of a smile but doubted it matched the exuberance tumbling around inside of her.

He walked her to the door, and she said good night, filled with the same elation as when her first book made the New York Times bestseller list.

19

Lila entered the old brick town hall building. She walked into the room to find a large, round table equipped with enough chairs for two dozen people.

After introducing herself to Anne Richards, the director, Lila pulled one of the blue plastic chairs away from the table and sat down. She recognized a few faces—her high school English teacher who told her how proud she was of her. Mrs. Bates, an old bridge partner of her mother's, waved a hello. Finally, Conrad's uncle Elmer, who was part of a lively discussion with Conrad, gave her a quick wink. He was the reason she was attending the meeting tonight. If she could book him for Saturday afternoon photo sessions at Window Shopping, Lila and Melanie were certain the store would enjoy a bump in sales.

Uncle Elmer was perfect for the role. The man was Santa's twin. In the five years that passed since she saw him last, his shock of dark hair had turned almost white, matching his barber-groomed beard. Although he was missing a round belly, pillow stuffing would do the job, but it was his jovial character that shined through to others. He not only resembled Santa, he bore the same mannerisms and charisma. How lucky for him to recognize his gifts during the most wonderful time of the year.

"Please take your seats everyone so we can get started," Anne instructed. "The first order of business is to welcome Lila Clark, who's filling in for Melanie

Winters during her medical leave."

Hands came together in soft applause.

Anne flashed a quick, courteous smile in Lila's direction. "Welcome, Lila, we're happy to see you here tonight."

"Thank you, everyone." Lila scanned the group, resting her eyes on Conrad, directly across from her. He appeared as if he anticipated a wonderful dinner at a posh restaurant. His attentiveness to those around him revealed a genuine interest in the animated conversation surrounding him. Lila instantly wished she'd chosen her seat with more care, but she dismissed the idea, realizing she'd stir up the gossip chain. The last thing Lila wanted was a scandal for her, Conrad, or Suzanne.

Once the meeting got underway, Lila found herself drifting. As she sipped her water and watched the clock, the new scone recipe waited for her attention back at the store. She voted with the group that the oversized ornaments were, indeed, a success and added Window Shopping to the list of businesses interested in joining the Ski Hill grand opening celebration. Finally, Mr. Drew, representing the Public Safety Department, reported that the plows were already working this year and ready for the winter season.

"Elmer, would you like to address the group and inform them of your services as Santa?" Anne switched gears.

Conrad's uncle rose. "Well, it's pretty simple. I can do pictures, read a story, or mill around your stores for a couple of hours, chatting with the customers. You tell me what you'd like, and I'll do it." He began to lower himself to the chair, but stopped midway. "Oh, and it's free of charge'" He smiled.

A round of applause followed.

"Thank you, Elmer, for that generous offer. I think that's pretty clear for everyone. I'd like a show of hands for all businesses interested in utilizing Elmer Hamilton's generosity this year."

Lila's hand was the first to shoot up into the air as if it were a kite caught up in a spring gust of wind.

Conrad snickered at her. Well, at least she was entertaining him, wasn't she?

Anne counted the raised hands under her breath. "Would those of you wishing to secure Mr. Hamilton as Santa see me so I can get your names and preferred days of the week? I'd like to post the schedule on our website. Thank you for coming, everyone. Our meeting is now adjourned, but do remember, our Christmas survey is next month, so please plan on a longer meeting."

Lila slipped on her jacket.

Conrad joined her. "Well, my uncle is certainly happy to be able to see you again, Lila."

She turned to face him. Every sense in her body switched over to high alert. "Oh, really? I hope he can fill me in on all the trouble you've managed to get yourself into over the last few years."

Conrad shot her a devilish grin. "Me? Come on, Lila."

"Well, if it isn't our Lila." The voice matched the face of one of Lila's favorite people in Conrad's family.

"How are you, Uncle Elmer?"

He shook his head as if he'd caught the error and didn't want it corrected. "It seems that I'll need to put on a few pounds in time for Christmas." He let out a *"Ho, ho, ho!"* to accentuate his point.

"Would you rather use a pillow? We can certainly fix you up with one."

"And deny me the luxury of eating too many Christmas cookies? No, thanks. So, you'd like Santa to come to the store? I noticed your hand was the first one raised."

"Did I appear overzealous?" Lila giggled. "Saturday afternoons would be a good fit for our customers."

"I agree. Say, Conrad here tells me he's finished with this ski chalet addition. Would it be all right if we stopped at the store on our way home so I can take a quick peek? If you remember, I taught him everything he claims to be good at these days."

Lila remembered the afternoons she and Conrad spent in his uncle's workshop. "I'd say that's perfectly OK. In fact, I'm headed there myself to stir together a batch of scones. But I need to touch base with Anne before I leave."

"We'll wait here and follow you down," Conrad said.

"Sounds good," Lila said and left the pair after spotting Anne across the room.

❄❄❄❄

Lila stood behind Conrad and his uncle in the chalet addition. Uncle Elmer gave a low whistle. "Well, well, well, this is something special." He followed Conrad from the addition back into the main store.

Lila stepped behind the counter. "Conrad did a great job, didn't he?"

Uncle Elmer nodded. "I could tell he was talented back when he was ten-years-old, and tonight I was

A Christmas Kind of Perfect

proven right."

Lila agreed. "Conrad thought of adding the mini-benches for the little people. He said he wanted a special place for them to congregate and enjoy themselves as much as their parents."

Uncle Elmer shifted his gaze over to Conrad with a proud smile. "That sounds like something you'd think of. You always had a way with kids." He turned to Lila. "I wish you could be there when Conrad walks through the door at one of our family get-togethers. The little guys run to him as if they're tacklers on a football field. It's great fun to watch."

Lila could imagine the scene. "Yes, I can believe."

Conrad's phone rang. Holding up one finger, he told them he needed to take the call.

"I'm glad he's found a measure of success in his work. I'm so proud of him," Uncle Elmer said.

Lila suspected Uncle Elmer's respect for Conrad matched hers. "He's good at what he does, but more importantly, I think he's built a reputation based on trust and reliability paired with excellent craftsmanship. People can count on him. If he says he'll be there, he shows up, and he finishes on time," Lila said.

Uncle Elmer shook his head. "A work ethic like that seems to be hard to find these days. I'm not sure why, but it is. And what about you, young lady? Running this store must be a whole lot different compared to writing books in New York."

"I've enjoyed running the store a lot more than I thought I would. It's a refreshing change, and it's given me a few ideas for my next book. In fact, I've started something brand new."

"Ever consider moving back?" He nodded slowly

as if to encourage her agreement to his idea.

Lila hoped the surprise didn't register on her face. Was he serious? "Here?"

"Why not?"

Lila flushed, heat running up her neck and coloring her cheeks. She busied her hands with a miniature statue of Joseph from a nativity scene. "No, I, ah…"

Conrad returned the phone to the holder. "Don't give her a hard time now, Uncle Elmer."

Uncle Elmer waved his hand in Lila and Conrad's direction. "Yeah, yeah, yeah. You kids never want to talk about the tough stuff, do you?"

He said it with a chuckle in his voice, but his words caused Lila to wonder if part of what he meant wasn't true.

Conrad turned to his uncle and thumbed toward the back of the room. "Listen, I'm going to shut things down back there. Thanks for coming down."

"You're welcome," Uncle Elmer said. "I'm proud of you, Conrad." He gave Conrad a bear hug.

Conrad returned the surprise affection with a couple of hefty pats on Uncle Elmer's arms.

Uncle Elmer turned to Lila. "Santa Claus will be here Saturday afternoon at one o'clock."

"Excellent. I can't wait to transition into Christmas," she said and walked him to the door.

After Uncle Elmer left, she turned off the lights and locked the door. The front part of the store grew dark. The amber light cast from a Tiffany lamp on the checkout counter illuminated Conrad and created an unexpected intimacy between them.

"I need to stir up a batch of scones for tomorrow. I'm trying to stay the course that Melanie put in place for me. We thought to switch it up a bit from cranberry to blueberry. There's a new recipe waiting for me in the kitchen." Was she rambling? A nervous tension stretched between them like a taut cable supporting two trees falling away from each other.

Conrad smiled. "Don't forget the cinnamon."

Lila frowned. "Cinnamon?" She was almost certain that wasn't on the list of ingredients. "I don't remember reading that in the recipe."

He cocked his head to the side and wore a mischievous grin. "It brings out the flavor of the blueberries."

"Are you serious?" Lila wasn't certain if he was legitimately sharing a baker's secret or playing with her the way he used to. Too many times in the past he'd gotten the best of her in a mistruth or real-life fable, only for the two of them to cut up laughing later.

Conrad grinned and held his ground. "Well, don't believe me, but they won't be as good. I can vouch for that. I'm a scone expert." He stood as if he taught a class on the subject.

"Oh, Conrad, you of all people realize what a nervous cook I am in the kitchen. If it's really important, tell me."

Conrad threw his head back in a boisterous laugh. "All right, I give up. I probably watched one of those famous chefs mention it on TV."

"OK, now you're pulling my leg. Do you mean to say that you watch cooking shows?"

He advanced toward her, placing his hands on the wall on each side of her and playfully smiling down at her as he used to years ago. "Only when I visit my mom, but I had you there for a minute, didn't I? You actually believed I watched cooking shows."

"I wouldn't put it past you. You probably do watch..."

Her hands landed on that same place they used to on his chest. Lila's eyes met his—the ones she'd fallen in love with so many years ago and again right now. She never thought it possible, but she found it again—loves. Their laughter faded. Their breath frantic and labored.

His lips brushed hers, first one way, and the other, in their familiar way she remembered oh, so well. Her resolve weakened right along with her knees. With his kiss, every year they'd been apart melted away. Her heartbeat pounded in her ears. She wrapped her arms around him as he cupped her face and kissed her cheeks, the top of her nose, her mouth, over and over again.

Restraint was gone. She could never be close enough to him. Conrad. Guided by her heart, she responded as she had so many years ago, with so much more meaning than with any other man. His touch awakened what she thought died so long ago.

Then Conrad stepped back, lowering his hands and looking away from her.

He didn't need to say a thing. They'd stepped over a line that shouldn't have been crossed.

Before he could explain, Lila pressed a finger across his lips. She didn't want his apology. Instead, she wanted him to tell her he was hers forever, but he couldn't do that, not yet.

Conrad lowered his head, his forehead resting against hers. "I need to get my life in order."

"Um-hmm," she agreed, realizing what he needed to do. But the thought wasn't given a chance to linger when his lips claimed hers all over again.

20

Lila was at the store, behind the counter checking out Mrs. McPherson, a loyal customer and a member of the Christmas choir when Elmer Hamilton, dressed as Santa, stepped in line as if he were the next customer.

"May I gift wrap this for you?" Lila asked Mrs. McPherson.

"Yes, please," Mrs. McPherson folded her arms across her chest, and Lila sensed she wasn't in the slightest hurry.

Lila wrapped the gift and then twirled and twisted glittered satin, creating a bow, and secured it with heavy-duty tape to the top of the box.

"Oh, how lovely. Thank you, dear. Are you staying here in Sister Bay for good? I'm sure Melanie could use the help after the babies arrive."

Lila shook her head. "No, Melanie's mother will be operating the store during her maternity leave, and I'll need to return to New York."

Mrs. McPherson wore a frown. "Oh, that's a disappointment."

The sting of letting one of Melanie's customer's down caught Lila's attention. But what could she do? Her life was in New York.

"There's so much noise in New York. Are you sure you want to go back?" Mrs. McPherson added.

Lila giggled at the woman's description of New York. "Well, unfortunately, it's where I live now."

"Too bad. You're a nice addition to the store. I'm

going to miss your smiling face and those blueberry scones. Whatever do you put in them that make them taste so good?"

Lila smiled, recalling it wasn't her secret, but Conrad's. More importantly, she remembered his soft kisses that night and his promise to straighten out his life. She was counting on the promise more than he realized. "Cinnamon," she said, bringing herself back to the moment. "It brings out the flavor of the blueberries."

The woman gasped. "No kidding. I can't say I've ever tried that. Thank you for sharing."

"Well, someone very dear to me told me about it, so the least I can do is pass it on." Lila placed the wrapped gift into one of the striped bags and handed it to the older woman, but not before dropping in the flyer for the Ski Hill grand opening ceremony.

"We hope you can make it to the grand opening ceremony for the Ski Hill. I placed a brochure in your bag to help remind you. Merry Christmas, Mrs. McPherson."

Mrs. McPherson accepted the bag and turned to leave. "I'll do my best. It seems to be the event of the season. Merry Christmas, Lila."

"I'd be willing to bet it's not the first time you've been asked that question." Uncle Elmer rounded the counter for a hug before Lila could give him a proper hello.

Lila snuggled into the velvety fabric of his embrace. "Actually, I do get that question from time to time."

Uncle Elmer shook his head. "I'm not surprised. You're one of those rare people in this world who possesses a special way with people, Lila. I saw it when you were dating Conrad all those years ago."

Lila smiled at his praise, uncertain if that was true. "Thank you for the kind words. I'm so glad you're here today. We've actually been getting phone calls reserving spots for all the children who want a visit with Santa."

"Your decision to start Santa visits the first week in December was smart. I've learned you've made decisions on other good ideas for the store, as well."

Lila's mouth fell open. "Really? From whom?"

Uncle Elmer patted his pillow-stuffed body. "Santa has his little helpers who are always watching, remember?"

"Oh, for goodness' sake. Of course. Well, whoever it is, I'm grateful for the compliment. It's important I do well for Melanie in her absence."

He placed a firm hand on her back and gave it a couple pats. "Lila, you don't impress me as a young woman who does a bad job at anything."

Lila shrugged. "I'm sorry, I can't agree with you there. I seem to manage to make a lot of bad decisions that end up hurting people."

"People? Or Conrad?"

Lila stopped and turned to face him. "How did you guess?"

Uncle Elmer chuckled. "Not by magic. Don't forget. I spent a lot of time with you two, years ago. I may be old, but I can still recognize the spark in both yours and Conrad's eyes."

"Well, he's destined for a whole different life now, isn't he?" Lila said rubbing a spot from the floor with her shoe.

"You mean with Suzanne?"

"Yes." She hated to admit it, but it was the truth.

Uncle Elmer laid a hand on Lila's shoulder quieting her preoccupation with the floor. "Can I give you some advice or better yet, a gift from Santa?"

Lila brought her hands to her chest, grateful for the shift to a lighter mood. "How could I refuse a present from Santa?"

Uncle Elmer set his toy bag on the floor and began riffling through it. "Now, where is it?" he asked himself as if he was searching for a gift intended especially for her. He smiled when he retrieved a gold-wrapped gift from the bag and placed it into Lila's open hands. "It's our dreams in life that help us stay alive. Anyone can understand by looking at your success you've reached the big dreams, but don't forget about the little ones. The very first dreams that were born with you. Oftentimes, they hold the most importance." He placed the box in her hands.

She could almost close her fingers around it. It was heavy but not so much so that she needed both hands to support it. Curiosity brewed, she couldn't imagine the contents. It was delicate and held enough meaning for him to want to give it to her along with his advice. She brought it in close to her heart.

"Thank you, Uncle Elmer. Whatever it is I'll cherish it always because it'll remind me of this special time in my life."

"You open it when the time is right, not necessarily on Christmas morning."

Lila turned her head slightly. "When is that?"

He began to scan the store. "I'm quite certain when that times arrives, you'll recognize it. Now where is Santa's chair?"

21

The second week in December found Lila standing on the sidewalk in front of the display window. She was doing her best to ignore the freezing rain that pricked the back of her neck. She shivered and wished she'd grabbed her coat. Her reflection in the glass was one of sheer determination. For the third time, she repositioned the chalkboard easel that read "Santa's Here Today" and of all things to happen next, the phone rang. *Oh no!*

If Melanie were still running the store, the decision to place the announcement board outside wouldn't be an issue because she'd have had it out there all morning. Unfortunately, Lila forgot all about it while she prepared for the upcoming Twelve Days of Christmas Sale. The idea to run a sale on each of the twelve days before Christmas came to her after enjoying the carol played on the radio. It wasn't as if she'd needed more to do. The problem was figuring out how to turn off the ideas for the store.

She was convinced the sale would pull customers into the store and double Christmas sales. Who doesn't love a discount during the holidays? Now that Melanie received a good report from her accountant, Lila wanted to help make deep inroads into the black. The only problem was her return trip to New York. She wanted to postpone, not by much, a week or two. That way she'd have the opportunity to run the Christmas Blues Sale, an idea that she woke up with this morning.

She never imagined running the store would give her so much satisfaction, but that's exactly what had happened.

Sprinting into the store, Lila tried to remember where she'd last placed the phone. It was now on the third ring. At least she thought of propping the door open with the umbrella stand, or the call may have switched over to voicemail. That was a big no-no in the small retail business.

She slowed her pace when she'd passed Santa's corner. This was Uncle Elmer's second Saturday in the store playing Santa, and so far, it helped sales. The last thing Lila wanted to do was to appear frazzled in front of him, the photographer, the little boy sitting on his lap, and the parents who appeared to be enjoying the visit as much as their son.

On the fourth ring, Lila reached the checkout counter. She brushed away the unused wrapping paper, scolding herself for not having a clean surface as Melanie preferred. If only she was more like Melanie, but the truth was she wasn't—not in the store or in the kitchen. She breathed a sigh of relief. The phone sat next to the tape dispenser, as if it belonged like a shaker of salt next to the pepper on a kitchen table.

Lifting the phone to her ear, she inhaled slowly and shifted her tone from panic to welcoming and answered the call. "Good morning, Window Shopping, this is Lila, how may I help?"

"It took you long enough. Did you misplace the phone again?"

Melanie caught her again! "Oh, Mel. I was working outside, and with my luck, the phone rings."

"Well, I'm awfully glad you answered it because…they're here." Melanie giggled on the other end.

Lila paused. Did this mean what she thought it meant? "Oh, my goodness. The babies? When? How? Are you OK?"

"Slow down, Lila. Yes, it happened last night. I hadn't felt well all day. I wasn't sure if it was my mother watching my every move or my husband asking if he could do anything for me. Bless their hearts."

Lila leaned against the counter, relief filling her. She placed a light hand over her rapidly beating heart. "Leave it up to you to find humor in labor."

"Maybe now but when the pains started coming in ten-minute increments, we headed right for the hospital. Four hours later, our boys came into the world."

Ooh, Lila couldn't wait to hold Mel's babies in her arms. "I'm so happy for you. Congratulations, Mel. I was so afraid I'd be back in New York before they were born. Who do they take after?"

"Benjamin has my dark hair and skin tone, but Brian is fair like his daddy. They're gorgeous, Lila, if I must say so myself."

Lila could sense the pride in her friend's voice. Even she couldn't believe the whole ordeal was over. "No doubt. And the labor, how did you manage?"

"With lots of medication. Benjamin was our first. He was a tough little bugger, but Brian was a piece of cake. Of course, he was smaller. I can't believe they're here. I'm a mother, Lila, a mother. I'm so happy, so ecstatically happy."

Lila shook her head fighting back her own tears of absolute joy. "And Jack?"

"He's beside himself. He's called everyone on his

list. He's telling perfect strangers now, like the janitor and visitors for other new moms up here. It's getting a little embarrassing."

Lila could picture the whole scene in her mind. She cried and laughed happy tears until they collected in the corners of her eyes. She wiped them away with her index finger. These are the blessing you receive when you follow God's lead and make the right decisions. Life would never be as it was for Melanie again. She'd left the past behind and walked boldly into the next chapter. Lila battled the sting of regret and wondered if she, too, could ever be so blessed.

"When can I visit?" Lila asked. She shoveled her dark thoughts to the side as if clearing away snow from the store's front entrance.

"Give me a couple of days. They told me once the meds wear off, I'll be in for a whole lot of pain."

"That works for me too. Tomorrow's Sunday, and Cathy and I go to church. On Monday, we start the Twelve Days of Christmas Sale, and Tuesday, well, you remember how maddening Tuesdays always are."

"You are a woman in charge, aren't you? Seriously, Lila, I'm glad you came back to the church. You're finding your center in life again, aren't you?"

"I am. Listen to this, Mr. Abbott gives me the nod if he needs me in the choir. I sing almost every week."

Melanie giggled. "Oh, I remember the official nod that tells you, 'Now you may join the choir,'" Melanie said in a vibrato effect.

"That's the cue all right," Lila couldn't control her giggles. She'd lost count of how often Melanie caused her to double over in laughter since coming home. Her happiness quotient was sky high. It was so good to be home again for so many reasons. Melanie and Conrad were at the top of that list.

The beep-beep-beep signaled an incoming call and interrupted them.

"Oh, oh, is that duty calling?" Melanie asked.

"Right. How's next Wednesday for a visit?"

"Perfect, I'll be home. I can't wait for you to come over."

"Give those babies a big kiss from Auntie Lila for me."

"With pleasure."

Lila said a quick good-bye and switched over to take the call. This time there was no need to feign a welcoming tone.

22

The days leading up to Lila's visit with Melanie gave Lila a chance to daydream what it must be like to bring a new life into the world. After leaving Sister Bay, she didn't give that idea much consideration. Now that she was near Conrad again, the thought entered her mind more often. In fact, Lila lost count of how many times she dreamed of becoming a wife and a mother. What power did Conrad have over her to cause these wanderings in her mind? Of course, Lila believed that nothing held as much meaning in life. A child produced from the love between a man and a woman was the ultimate gift a couple could give to one another.

A rare lull in the store gave Lila the opportunity to gaze out the display window for the one hundredth time. A fresh snow was falling which appeared like confetti on a birthday cake. Why did her moods shift from excitement for Melanie to melancholy for herself these last couple of days? It didn't take her long to figure that out—because she wanted a husband, a baby, and a family all her own as much as she desired her first bestseller.

Oh, how thing change in life.

She prayed that one day she too would experience the opportunity to place a child in Conrad's arms. She anticipated the love on his face—pure joy. Lila sighed. She believed the plan for her life was already in motion. Was it too late for her and Conrad? The sermon last Sunday reminded her that behavior follows beliefs. Letting go and trusting always was the tough part for her.

Outside a snowy gust caught hold of the awning. It flapped like one of her mother's sheets hanging on a clothesline in the summer wind. Lila jerked back to the present. "Stop your daydreaming and close up," she scolded herself. Within the next hour, she made two stops—to pick up gifts for the boys and a quick stop to the florist for flowers for Melanie. With a renewed spirit, she was turning onto Melanie's street when her phone signaled a new text. She pulled over to the curb and read the incoming message.

Great news. Call me. It was from Andrea.

"Better to do it now," Lila said under her breath and dialed Andrea's number. She picked up on the first ring. "Andrea, hi, it's Lila, how are things?"

"Perfect. Excellent. I couldn't be happier—for you, that is. You're going to love what I'm about to tell you."

Lila held her breath, unsure Andrea was right. So much change happened for her it was almost as if she were living two lives.

"OK, I'm listening," Lila said, forcing an upbeat tone. Whatever good news Andrea wanted to tell her already had a different ring to it now. Somewhere along the way, the music changed for Lila, and she was dancing to another tune.

"With a lot of encouragement and a good push, Jim pitched you to the editors at the new publishing house."

Lila shifted the vehicle into park, allowing the car to idle. Andrea's voice slipped into its squeaky, I'm-excited range.

"No kidding." Lila was stunned. She brought her thumbnail between her teeth. Did Andrea mention to her that Jim was planning on doing that, and she flat out forgot?

"They want to meet you and listen to your ideas for your next book series. Its crunch time over there for their next season, so there's no time to waste. We need to move quickly."

"When?" Lila asked. She hoped it wouldn't be before Christmas.

"Next Friday. If you make the impression I believe you will, you'll be all set for the next three years. You'll be busy. No more vacations."

"Is that the twenty-third?" Lila said as if she'd misheard. It would mean she'd miss Christmas in Sister Bay.

"That's what we talked about, remember? You coming home Christmas week?"

Lila twirled a lock of her hair around a finger. She suspected asking to postpone the meeting until after the holidays would be like telling a child he couldn't eat the Christmas cookies on the platter in front of him. She'd run out of time. *Oh, Conrad.*

"This is the break we were hoping for. We've got to move forward on this if you want to successfully switch genres. Lila, you need to come home."

Maybe she shouldn't have told Andrea about her new series so soon. She hoped Andrea couldn't sense her hesitation but the thought of returning to her empty apartment dampened her spirit. "I'll do my best."

"Well, you'd better. I ran myself ragged getting you this appointment. And may I add, to satisfy your desire for change. Listen, I've got to run. Believe it or not, I've picked up two more clients, and they've got me hopping from one thing to the next. I hope it's an easy flight."

After Lila disconnected the call, she tossed her phone against her purse sitting on the passenger seat.

"I hate these things," she yelled. She slipped the gear into drive and continued down the street to Melanie's house. She pushed the conversation from her thoughts, parked the car, and made her way up the walk. After a light knock, she tweaked the door open, managing to balance two dozen roses and the babies' gifts in her arms. Her purse, minus her phone, was slung over her shoulder.

Melanie was seated on the sofa and placed a finger across her lips as she urged Lila closer. She was nursing one of the boys. The other lay sleeping in a wicker basket nearby. "Oh, my goodness, you've outdone yourself again. Did you buy out the florist? Come in and sit down next to me."

Lila slipped off her shoes and coat and laid the flowers and gifts on a nearby table. She took a seat next to Melanie and lowered her gaze at the infant in her friend's arms, snuggled tight against Melanie's breast.

"Say hello to Brian. I'm sorry but you missed Jack by ten minutes. He ran to the grocery store for us. The poor thing, he's tired himself out doing everything around here when I was restricted to bedrest." Melanie brushed a finger across her new son's feathery head.

The scent of baby filled the space like a fresh rain. The sound of a mother's heartbeat coming from a brown teddy bear in the bassinet repeated, *thump-thump, thump-thump.*

"He's so beautiful," Lila said, fighting an

overwhelming urge to cry. The news from Andrea, so upsetting moments ago, faded in the presence of Melanie and her newborns.

"Benjamin decided he was too sleepy to wait for you. I fed him, and his daddy snuggled him in a cuddle that worked its magic. Look at the results."

Lila's gaze followed Melanie's to Benjamin. His gentle breathing sounding like a soft melody. Soon she was mesmerized with the easy rise and fall of the sleeping infant's chest. She would be content to stay right where she was and watch him sleep for a long time.

"There's a pot of tea on the stove if you're interested."

"Thank you, but I'm fine." Although tea sounded delicious, Lila couldn't pull her attention from the newborns.

"Conrad was here earlier," Melanie said, pulling Lila out of her thoughts.

Lila followed Melanie's gaze toward the two giant panda teddy bears in the corner. Fighting a pang in her heart she said, "I expected he'd come."

"How's it going between you two?"

Lila shrugged. "Since he's finished the ski chalet, there's little opportunity to run into him. It's been almost a week."

Melanie's face softened. "Your eyes tell all, Lila."

Lila rubbed the palms of her hands together. "I'll admit it. I miss him. The last time we spoke he told me he wanted to get his life in order, but so far, nothing. Is it possible things changed for him?"

"I doubt that." Melanie shifted her weight on the cushion. She took in a sharp breath.

Lila offered her hands in Melanie's direction. "Are

you OK?"

Melanie wrinkled her nose. "I'm fine." As she moved again to make herself comfortable, the baby in her arms appeared content and undisturbed. "It's the healing process now that's a little tough."

"What can I do?"

"Believe me," Melanie said, "I wish there was something you could do. But, Lila, I really don't think Conrad is second-guessing anything, especially when it concerns you. He's a considerate, thoughtful man. He's probably waiting for the right time to come clean with Suzanne."

"Well, I'm not pushing him. If he's torn, maybe we're not meant to be together after all." Lila allowed her words to settle in between them. "Andrea just called," she said intentionally changing the subject.

Melanie threw her head back. "Good grief, can't that woman ever leave you alone?"

Lila snickered at Melanie's uncharacteristic response. "You'd like her. You're both gutsy, spirited women and whose opinion I value. Anyway, I spoke with her right before coming over here. She wants me back in New York by next Friday."

"Oh, Lila. No," Melanie moaned. "You can't leave before Christmas. That's ridiculous."

Lila shrugged. "That was our agreement, remember? And, she's worked hard lining up an important meeting for me, but to be honest, I don't want to go. I never thought it would happen, but my priorities changed."

Melanie adjusted the hand knit blanket around the baby in her arms. "That makes two of us. I think you need to give Conrad a chance to sort everything out with Suzanne. Can't you find a way to postpone until after the holidays? Who's expected to work during Christmas?"

Lila worked her toes into the cream-colored carpet. "And give what excuse? What about my commitments to people back in New York?"

"There are new responsibilities here, too. Blame it on me if you must and explain to Andrea that I need you at the store. Tell her about the sales we're running and Ski Hill's grand opening ceremony coming up. Buy yourself some time."

Lila rubbed the back of her neck. "This is the life I've carved out for myself. I can't abandon my career."

Melanie's nostrils flared. "Lila, are you seriously going to walk out on Conrad again?"

Lila buried her face in her hands. What was the answer? "I'm so torn. I've been praying for a sign to lead me in the right direction, but so far, nothing. Andrea needs me back in New York, and as far as I can determine, Conrad's still with Suzanne."

Melanie stretched out a free hand, and Lila grabbed on as if she were floating out to sea. Melanie was the life preserver that would save her.

"That's your sign not to leave. Be patient and find out how things work out here first."

Lila exhaled. The whole mess exhausted her.

"Try to push Andrea off until the week after Christmas."

Lila realized before she answered that the end of her trip was about to come to pass. "I'm not going to get away with that." She offered Melanie a wavering smile.

Melanie exhaled a long, drawn out breath. "Maybe what you need is a little Christmas magic. After all, you do have a direct line to Santa."

Lila slumped her shoulders in disbelief. "Oh, Mel, you're one of a kind. I'll do my best. OK?"

"OK," Mel said with a satisfied grin. She leaned toward Lila. "Now hold your godson for me."

Lila beamed a Christmas smile, as if she'd been presented with the gift she'd been waiting for all year. "My godson?" She opened her arms and Melanie placed the baby inside of them.

"That is if you're willing to take on another responsibility in life?" Melanie raised her eyebrows and tilted her head.

Lila forced her attention from the baby to Melanie. "Are you kidding? I wouldn't give that privilege up for anything."

"Not even another bestseller?" Melanie tapped her cheek with her slender finger.

Lila held back tears watching Brian struggle with a yawn. "Nope. Not even for that."

23

Despite the twenty-degree temperature, Lila stood outside the store in front of the display window staring at the Christmas scene she'd created. With three days left before Christmas Eve, she wanted to present a festive setting to draw customers into the store. *Toot-toot-toot*. Lila recognized the sound of Conrad's horn. She placed her hand over her heart to slow the beats and turned to watch him ease his monster truck alongside the curb.

He rolled down the window and rested his arm on the door as if it were eighty degrees outside. "How are things going?" he asked.

The sound of his voice set her feet in motion toward him. A hot flush washed over her. She wanted to invite him into the store for a cup of coffee but accepted that couldn't happen now. He'd finished the addition and moved on to his next job. Lila hoped the reason for his visit was to tell her he ended his relationship with Suzanne. She forced her attention to the display window, "Did I overdo it?"

He shrugged a shoulder. "Ahh…I'm not sure."

Lila threw her head back and laughed. "Men. You don't see life through the same lenses women do."

"I guess not. I've brought you something this morning. I think you'll like it." His voice hinted at mischief.

Lila lifted her eyebrows. "Me?" she asked and walked over to the driver's side of his truck.

He handed her a small white bag, which she opened the minute it hit her hands.

A round chocolate donut sat in the middle of the bag surrounded by white baker's tissue.

"I figured you haven't lost your taste for those little devils."

"And devils they are, but you're as guilty as I am for tempting me with them. Thank you," she said with a tilt of her head. She would much prefer thanking him properly by leaning into his truck and kissing him square on the lips. The smolder in his eyes told her he wanted to do the same. But her aunt scolded her once before that some people noticed them together, and Lila was determined to kill the gossip. Lila tore her eyes away from his, sensing an immediate loss of connection.

"You're welcome. It's good to see you." His voice was as smooth as the chocolate icing on the donut she held in her hand.

"And you." Should she ask about Suzanne?

"Are you going to the dress rehearsal Thursday night for the Christmas concert?"

"Dress rehearsal?" she asked. It was hard to believe that was on his mind.

He blinked. "I mean the last choir practice."

Lila's heart sank. She should tell him about Andrea's call. "I am."

"Need a ride?" he asked under his breath. He wore the irresistible face of a naughty boy. Lila fought the urge to reach out and smack him.

She adjusted her sweater to keep her hands busy and her attention distracted from him. "I don't think that's a good idea for us to be alone together in your truck, do you?"

He shrugged, hiding a grin. "I s'pose not."

A sense of melancholy filled her. "I'm really going to miss all of this. I've been forcing myself to think about returning home to my apartment."

"I thought you were home." His comment cut to the quick.

She didn't want to, but she had to say it. "I mean New York."

Conrad jerked his arm into the truck. If he was trying to hide his aggravation, he wasn't succeeding. "I understood what you meant."

Lila stiffened. "Andrea called and asked that I come back to attend a meeting on Friday."

He banged the palm of his hand against the steering wheel. "Why is this beginning to seem like five years ago?"

His question threw Lila off track. He didn't even give her a chance to explain. Her mouth went as dry as the powdered sugar she dusted on her scones. She sensed that old wall erecting between them. The barricade she thought she'd dismantled brick by brick.

"What do you mean?" She tightened her grip on the bag unsure where to go with her response to his question.

"You running off to the big city. Is that how this is going to end between us?" He squared his face to hers and stared her straight in the eye. "Again?"

Did he sneer at her? Of all the nerve. One of Lila's gears shifted deep inside like turning on the Kitchen Aid mixer to maximum speed. "Conrad, I'm not sure what you expect me to do. We both carry responsibilities to other people who rely upon us to come through. Yours are here. Mine are in New York."

Conrad rapped his hands three times against the

door panel. "You're right. You've got yourself a big fancy career to take care of." He wiggled his thumb in her direction as if doling out a scolding and shifted his gaze to his wrist watch. "Got to run."

He pulled away from the curb before she could say good-bye. She watched the red truck roar through the yellow caution light and disappear from sight. Why was it that men thought speeding helped? It was about as helpful as losing your temper. And he was angry? *You've got to be kidding.* She was the one who should be furious. He was one step away from the altar—an almost-fiancé. He was aware all along what her plans were. To accuse *her* of running off? Who did he think he was? He'd given her no notification that he'd sorted things out. Did he think she was going to wait forever while he waffled?

Lila whirled around and stomped her way back to the store. The frustration bubbling over inside of her was like pulling out a tray of burnt scones from the oven. She surveyed the store deciding what needed a good cleaning. The collector Christmas bulbs always seemed to attract dust. She could certainly use a second batch of chocolate chip scones for Ski Hill's grand opening ceremony. Or how about the coffee machine? It could probably use a thorough vinegar scrub. She wasn't going to let the argument with Conrad ruin a perfect start to the day. But as her heart sank, she already realized the damage was done.

She walked into the store and flipped on the music. A Christmas song roared to life, rattling antique teacups on saucers. "Of all the nerve," she spat and marched back to the kitchen, fighting the urge to pick a fight with Andy Williams singing, "It's the Most Wonderful Time of the Year."

❄❄❄❄

Exhausted by day's end, Lila busily marked down Christmas cookie platters for the next day's sale. She'd wanted to finish the job before closing up for the night.

The door opened, and Lila turned to greet her customers.

Suzanne held the door open for her mother before they both stepped into the store.

Lila placed the pen down on the counter. "You can handle this," she whispered and went to greet them. "Hello, ladies, may I be of assistance?"

Suzanne wore a long red coat and one of the most beautiful mink hats Lila ever laid eyes on. Blond coppery strands of hair fell loosely around her face. She could easily have doubled as a Russian princess.

"We're searching for something special for my father's sixty-fifth birthday tomorrow. Mother insisted on coming here."

Lila picked up on Suzanne's icy undercurrent. She recalled the advice Melanie shared with her on handling difficult customers. Although she wouldn't consider the Matthews problematic, this sale would definitely be a challenge.

Lila inhaled to the count of three. "I understand. Is he a collector of fine things?"

"How did you guess?" Mrs. Matthews asked as she returned an antique steam train engine to the shelf. A much older version of Suzanne peered back at her. Lila noticed the same exquisite green eyes and high sculpted cheekbones that settled to create an attractive full face.

"Call it intuition," Lila said attributing her sense

when Mrs. Matthews chose the collector's train, one of their rare and lavishly detailed pieces from a limited edition.

Lila raised her eyebrows. "Is he fascinated with steam trains?"

Mrs. Matthews wrinkled her petite nose, her hair holding an intricately coiffed style. "No, not really, but he could be. He respects items from his past—for instance, coins, skeleton keys, and even marbles. I wouldn't be surprised to find a few rare stamps in his possession."

Lila paused, inventorying the store's offerings. "I'd like to show you something over in jewelry that may be a perfect fit." She led the pair over to a small selection of maple keepsake boxes. A centered gold plate offered the option for engraving.

Mrs. Matthews covered her mouth with a hand and took a small intake of breath.

Lila lifted the largest box from the shelf. "This gift appeals to those who value heirlooms, a keepsake, or other treasures they wish to protect from harm or loss. They're called keepsake boxes and for good reason as they pair the sense of an exotic treasure chest with an air of elusiveness."

"Oh, my. Would you open it please? I'd like to peer inside," Mrs. Matthews asked.

Lila smiled, her sales instincts leading her into a promising sale. "Of course, allow me." Lila turned the brass key adorned with a golden tassel until it clicked. Holding the box against her body, she slowly drew the hinged cover toward her, allowing the ladies a view inside at the burgundy-velvet-lined interior.

"This is perfect, Mother," Suzanne breathed, as if she was surprised the store was able to produce something of value for her father's birthday.

Mrs. Matthews beamed and a smile of satisfaction spread across her lovely face. "I agree. We'll take it."

"I thought you might like it. Would you be interested in having the plate engraved?"

"We'd need it by tomorrow night, but it's only three initials. Is that possible?" Mrs. Matthews laid a slender finger alongside her face.

"I'll personally drive it down to Albright Jewelers. Mr. Albright insists on doing all of our engraving himself. I'll make sure the box is ready by tomorrow afternoon."

Once behind the counter, Lila rang up the purchase and accepted the credit card from Mrs. Matthews. She was unwinding enough wrapping paper, included with the sale, when the conversation between mother and daughter caught her attention.

"You should register down here for wedding gifts." Mrs. Matthew's eyes roamed the shelves behind the counter.

"I suppose so," Suzanne said in an exhale as if she were agreeing to go on a blind date.

Suzanne's face didn't hold the excitement of a bride-to-be but rather one of disinterest or possibly boredom. Was it plausible she didn't care whether Conrad proposed or not? Lila twirled metallic ribbon around her hand and slipped it into the bag. Her earlier suspicions about their relationship ringing clear. There might be a chance for her and Conrad, after all. She forced her attention back to her task and reassured mother and daughter their keepsake box would be waiting for them tomorrow at Albright Jewelers as promised.

After they left the store, Lila tidied up, closed the

shop, and headed to the jewelers. She hoped there was time to share a late supper with Aunt Cathy. She needed her sound advice after what she'd witnessed with the Matthews. The argument between her and Conrad needed resolution, too. They needed to talk.

As Lila made her way across the street to the jewelers, she considered Melanie's suggestion to try and postpone the meeting. After sharing the details with Mr. Albright, he assured her the box would be ready for pick up tomorrow afternoon. In fact, he promised he'd call the Matthews and inform them himself when the box was ready.

Fifteen minutes later, Lila hustled across the street to her car. She slipped her key into the ignition. A cold blast of air hit her square in the face. Her nerves were on edge. Was it the argument's fault or Suzanne's disposition? She was rubbing her palms together, waiting for the car to warm up, when her biggest fear came true. Conrad was walking toward the jewelry store. Her breath caught. Was that Conrad—for sure? She scanned down the street. His red truck was parked a block from the store.

She rubbed her eyes hoping for clarity to a different truth. He pulled the door open and walked into the jewelry store. So he'd decided to go ahead with the proposal, after all. She nibbled on her bottom lip, and despite her best efforts, an avalanche of tears fell down her face, blurring her vision. Minutes passed as Lila waited and prayed that he'd turn around and walk right back out of that store. But he didn't. Every bone in her body ached. For a moment, she thought she'd be sick. She lowered her head and gripped the steering wheel. She wept for all that was lost—her future with the love of her life. When her tears came to an end, she blew her nose and dried her eyes.

She remembered her Sunday school lessons where she'd learned that if you ask, God will always answer your prayers, but not necessarily with the answer you hoped for. Was this the sign she'd been praying for? She reminded herself to let go, to trust, and to follow.

This was the possibility that always lurked in the dark that meant she needed to go home. She shifted the gear into drive and realized it was time to return to New York.

Lila turned into the driveway at Aunt Cathy's. Although the commute home wasn't long, it provided her enough time to settle her emotions down and for her tears to dry. She noticed a soft amber light cast from a lamp in the kitchen window. That usually meant her aunt went to bed early. Although she wanted to tell her aunt about Suzanne, in a way, Lila was relieved for their conversation to wait a day. Aunt Cathy was aware that she'd booked the flight back to New York when Andrea called last week, but she'd been fighting the idea with Lila ever since. Now that Lila was certain of Conrad's intentions toward Suzanne, there was little reason to make that call to Andrea and ask for more time. Everything changed the moment Conrad walked into Albright's. She shared as much with Melanie on the drive home. That wasn't an easy conversation, either.

After hanging up her coat and slipping off her boots, Lila walked into the kitchen. A sticky note was pressed onto the cooktop. *Supper's in the oven, off to bed early.* A heart drawn around Aunt Cathy's name ended the message. Lila smiled, realizing she was sure to miss the closeness they shared. She scanned the kitchen as if for the last time and compared her life here with that of

New York, uncertain she wanted to make the transition back.

She opened the oven door and lifted the foil off the warming plate. Underneath, she found a meatloaf dinner that smelled heavenly and matched any tapas grill she enjoyed in Manhattan. Thick red sauce speckled with horseradish covered the entrée. A small serving of mashed potatoes with a dollop of butter was placed next to a scoop of homemade baked beans. The sight made her mouth water and her eyes glisten. Her stomach growled. After the fight with Conrad, she'd lost her appetite, and her enthusiasm for the day right along with it. Now, she was famished and exhausted. Using a hot pad, she lifted the plate from the oven and poured herself a cup of chamomile tea from the pot sitting on the back burner. She turned on the television to the weather station for company.

For the next twenty minutes, she tried to enjoy her dinner—her appetite often weakened when she was upset, and Conrad had done a bang-up job on turning her world upside down today. Her attention piqued as she listened to the predictions of "significant snowfall" in the forecast. Her stomach tightened. She would have to leave earlier than planned to beat the snow.

She curled and uncurled her toes in the air, releasing the tension in her feet after a full day's work. Oh, how she'd love a foot massage right about now. That was one of the perks of living in a city like Manhattan—you could find anything your heart desired—anything but love. That was especially true for Lila since her true love—the love of her life—was right here in Sister Bay.

When she was finished, she scrubbed her dishes clean, turned off the television, snapped off the lights, and climbed the stairs to her room. She hoped—no, she prayed—she'd get some rest. All she wanted to do now was close her eyes and sleep.

24

Conrad drove a little too fast on his way to Albright's. Lila ticked him off—royally. He found the woman exasperating. His mind reeled backward to the incident with the flooring. By walking through the door, she managed to topple over his entire stack of laminate, which interrupted his workflow.

Thanks to her, he was forced to attend a book signing. There were only a half dozen or so guys in the room—probably dragged there by their wives—and he was one of them. And to top it all off, Suzanne showed up after claiming she wouldn't be there. That turned out to be a two-day argument.

He was willing to bet that his mother would never have asked him to sing in the Christmas choir if Lila hadn't come back into the picture. They'd gotten along like a mother and daughter right from the start. Now that he was thinking about it, Conrad smelled something fishy. It was probably a setup from the beginning.

After everything that happened between them, Lila told him yesterday that she was returning to New York. Well, if that was what she wanted, so be it. As soon as she was gone, he and Suzanne could get back into their regular routine. He pulled into a parking stall a block away from Albright Jewelers and killed the engine. His stomach clenched. He shouldn't have eaten when his nerves were on edge. In the quiet, Conrad watched the oversized snowflakes collect on his windshield. He sucked in a gulp of air, grabbed the door handle, and fought the urge to run.

Conrad walked into Albright Jewelers with a heart as heavy as a bag of cement and a reignited anger. Now that he thought about it, it was his plan all along to marry Suzanne. He was running out of time, and Suzanne wasn't the patient type. She'd dropped enough hints, sent him love e-mails during the week, and forced herself into the kitchen. He got the message. It was time he proposed. He didn't blame her, and when she referred to their relationship as perpetual dating, she was right.

Yet, the need for more certainty ate away at him. Either she was the woman he wanted to walk through life with or she wasn't. She appeared certain of him, but the pause came from his gut. His buddies told him it was cold feet. They'd all went through the same. There were times Conrad noticed even they shared Suzanne's point of view and asked him, "What's taking so long?"

He joined his hands behind his back and inched toward the glass counter. Bending at the waist, he peered down at the stones that sparkled up at him. Jack Albright slowly approached. He was nearing his seventieth birthday, but he still opened up the store every day Monday through Saturday. Last year, he'd hired Conrad to install a copper tin awning in honor of fifty years in business. He said he wanted to catch the reflection of the sunsets because it reminded him of his diamonds—each one unique and breathtaking in their own way. That was enough to convince Conrad that when the time came to buy a diamond, he'd be coming to Albright's.

From behind the counter, Mr. Albright faced him.

A Christmas Kind of Perfect

"Well, Mr. Hamilton, I figured I'd have the pleasure of serving you soon."

Conrad's brow furrowed. "Oh?"

"The missus told me she spotted you around town with someone very special and a big smile across your face. She said, 'Jack, it's a matter of time before that young man is at your store buying one of your fancy diamonds.'"

"You don't say. Well, I, ah—"

Mr. Albright wore a gentle smile. "I tell you what. Why don't you allow me to get things started for you? What's the lady's preference—white or yellow gold? White gold has been the preferred choice for the last few years, but if she likes yellow, I can accommodate that as well."

Conrad shrugged, realizing he lacked the proper preparation.

"Are you familiar with the three Cs?"

The corners of Conrad's mouth twitched. "No, sir, I can't say that I am."

"There's three aspects to consider in a diamond—cut, color, and clarity. Let me pull out a couple of cases for you. Did you have an idea about the size of the stone you'd like for her? Today, most are a carat, but we can go up from there. Of course, it gets pricey when we do that."

Conrad flexed his fingers into his palms. This wasn't going to be as easy as he'd thought.

Mr. Albright rubbed his chin with a slender finger. "Years ago, your little lady used to babysit for us. Kids loved her. She played all kinds of games with them. After the kids went to bed, she picked up the house, too."

As far as Conrad could remember, Suzanne never

babysat unless her parents forced the issue and made her do it. "Are you sure about that?"

Mr. Albright gave Conrad a curt nod. "Oh, yes, Lila was our first choice. It's not something a father forgets."

Conrad's gut took a hit. "Lila?"

Mr. Albright smiled widely. "That's right."

Conrad's mouth went dry while his heart picked up speed. He ran a finger along the inside of his collar.

"Son, are you all right? You're a little green around the gills."

Conrad waved a hand in protest. "No, no. I'm OK, thank you. I need a minute."

"You're not the first to get squeamish about all of this. It's a big step asking a woman to marry you. You've got to get it right." He gave Conrad a nudge forward with his head as if to reassure Conrad everything would be OK.

Conrad placed his hands on the glass case in front of him and steadied himself. "I've got to get it right," he repeated. The truth hit him with such a force it was as if he'd jumped into Lake Michigan with that crazy Polar Bear Club on New Year's Day. It was as clear to him as the emerald cut diamond his eyes were fixed on. He understood, without a doubt, exactly what he was going to do. "That's the one." He pointed.

He lifted his gaze into the smiling eyes of Mr. Albright. "Good choice," he said and withdrew the ring from the case.

Thirty minutes later, Conrad walked out of the store, rubbing his thumb against the blue velvet box he held in his hand.

25

It was almost one o'clock in the afternoon when Conrad could get away and meet Suzanne for a light lunch at Sister Bay Bowl. He removed his jacket and hung it on one of the pegs near the door. It wasn't unusual for them to run into friends or family at the bowling alley, which added a few good laughs and lively conversation. Conrad doubted that would happen today. As he scanned the room for her, he remembered the good times when their relationship was brand new. Suzanne was the woman who took his mind off of Lila.

"Conrad, over here." Suzanne waved from a table near one of the large picture windows.

Conrad's feet were as heavy as if he'd strapped fifty-pound weights onto them. He kissed her lightly on the cheek and took a seat next to her.

She sipped from tall glass of iced tea. He watched her, realizing that every time he met up with her, she never failed to enchant him and everyone else in the room.

"You're as lovely as always, Suzanne."

She eyed him under thick lashes. "Not so bad yourself,"

He shifted in his seat under her scrutiny.

"You'll never believe where I went yesterday."

"Probably not," Conrad said after he ordered an iced tea from the waitress.

"Window Shopping."

Her tone was meant to surprise him, and it worked. He hoped his face remained neutral, although he was never good at playing cards because he didn't have a poker face.

"Mother insisted we give the store a try for Dad's birthday present, and she was right. We found the perfect gift. By the way, I assume you're coming to the party, right? Half the county's coming. Mother's hired a caterer and a disc jockey. It should be quite the bash. I don't think you're going to want to miss it." She took a small sip from her iced tea and waited for his response.

"Ah…" Conrad mumbled. He came here today for one reason, and he honestly wanted to get it over with. He wasn't prepared to talk about anything else.

"Mom suggested that I register for wedding gifts at Window Shopping—when the time is right, of course. She loves the store, but personally, I never cared for it. I'll do it to keep her happy."

Another hint for a proposal. Conrad's stomach lurched.

"I think it'd be a whole lot easier if we went together. Now don't worry, I understand your outlook on shopping, but I'll make it—"

"Suzanne." The pained look in her eyes at the tone of his voice was immediate. Did she sense what was coming?

She placed her glass down and twirled a painted fingernail around the rim.

Conrad lowered his gaze. "We need to talk something through here."

Her mouth dropped its smile. She slipped her bottom lip between her teeth, a habit he'd recognized when she grew uneasy.

Conrad stared at the indoor-outdoor carpeting beneath his feet. He shook his head from side to side. "I've been giving us a lot of thought these past few weeks. I'm not sure what to say—I mean, I don't think we're going to…"

"It's because of her, isn't it?" Suzanne surprised him as she slid her chair away from the table and stood as rigid as a piece of lumber.

Conrad hoped they weren't headed in the direction of an argument like the one they had a few weeks ago but anything was possible with Suzanne. She'd create a scene that would cause a gossip chain for weeks if her heart was headed in that direction.

"Suzanne, please sit down."

To his surprise, she did. She held her chin high. Her exotic green eyes that once held him captive now were as cold as ice.

"Actually, there's something I wanted to talk to you about, too. Would you mind if I went first?" She was coming from a place of strength now, not weakness. Conrad recognized the shift in her demeanor after being exposed to it many times through their business transactions. Her strategic and calculating mind was part of the reason for her enormous success. "Not at all. You go right ahead," Conrad said. He drew a long swallow from his tea, set the glass on the coaster, and turned his attention back to Suzanne.

"What I need to say is a little awkward, but I think it's time I come clean. You remember me talking about Bud, the corporate guru who came to teach us some new marketing strategies?"

Conrad lifted his gaze and locked eyes with Suzanne.

She pulled in a breath and squared up her shoulders. "He's quite the accomplished realtor, and our personalities click. Do you understand my meaning? He's opening up an enormous office in Madison, taking half of our office with him. He wants me at the helm. It's the break I've been waiting for."

Although she tried to conceal it, Conrad heard the crack in her voice, the pull of air into her lungs. She needed to get the words out. But what almost killed him, were the tears she was fighting. This was so unexpected. But then, they both understood what was really going on here. "I know how much your career means to you."

She pushed her glass away from her to the center of the table. "Oh, good. I was hoping you'd agree. So, you're OK with us taking some time apart to figure things out?"

Conrad gazed at the slender hand that slipped into his. He rubbed his callused thumb across her knuckles, realizing it would be the last opportunity he'd repeat the endearment. "If that's what you think is best."

She tilted her head toward him. Her face softening, "Now what is it that you wanted to talk to me about?"

Conrad shook his head. "It's not important. It can wait."

She withdrew her hand and stood up from the table. It broke free from his embrace like a kite string through his fingers. He understood the meaning. She was gone.

"Now, if you don't mind, I promised my mother I'd stop by and help her with the party decorations. I can see from here it's started snowing outside, so I'd like to get over there before the roads turn messy."

Conrad got to his feet and helped Suzanne on with her coat. He squeezed her shoulders.

"I loved our time together. I wish you only happiness," he whispered in her ear. He hoped she believed him because it was true.

She turned to face him. The teary-eyed woman of a moment ago was gone. She stood with a resolve that impressed him. "I'm going to be fine. I'll bury myself in my work and take Bud up on his offer, but would you accept some advice from someone who loved you?"

Conrad's ears perked at the past tense affection. He cast his gaze down at his feet. He wasn't sure what to expect but prepared himself for what he deserved.

She slid on her ebony black leather gloves as if it was any other day and not what it was—the end of them. "Don't wait this time. Go after her."

Conrad's jaw dropped. She knew.

Their eyes met and held. In the next moment, in the elegant style he'd grown accustom to, she leaned toward him. Her long blond hair falling forward, the exotic scent of her perfume filling the space. She brushed his cheek with a kiss as soft as the skin of one of Melanie's newborn sons. "Good-bye, love." Without another word, she turned and walked away.

26

Yesterday had been difficult. It was her final day at the store. She would miss being a part of Window Shopping.

Lila found Aunt Cathy in the kitchen reading the newspaper. She set it aside when Lila entered the room and sipped from her mug of coffee.

"You look awful. Did you sleep at all?" her aunt asked.

Lila yawned. "Not much." She pulled the sides of her robe together and tied the sash. It was a rough night despite her conviction not to dwell on everything that happened. She noticed her aunt wasn't dressed in her typical pink furry robe and slippers. "Where are you off to today?"

"I got a call from Melanie yesterday. She asked if I could help her mother out at the store this afternoon, especially with your Twelve Days of Christmas Sale. That's why I turned in early last night. I need all the stamina I can muster."

Lila shuffled into the room. "It's Christmas cookie platters today."

Her aunt raised her brows.

"Buy one, get one half off." Lila hoped to satisfy her aunt's question.

"I'm not talking about the sale." Aunt Cathy's tone told Lila that she meant business.

Aunt Cathy took a deep inhale, "Are you flying out today?"

"I'm taking that afternoon flight to LaGuardia."

Cathy raised her voice a notch. "Did you hear they're predicting four-to-six inches of snow?"

"I watched the news last night. The storm isn't moving in until later this afternoon. Plus, the sport utility vehicle has four-wheel drive. I'll be all right. I do not want you to worry about me." She was feigning a courage she didn't possess but the last thing she wanted was to worry her aunt.

"I wish you never made that flight reservation last week when your agent called."

"After what I witnessed last night, it's a blessing I did."

Cathy motioned for Lila to join her at the table. "Sit down a minute and tell me what happened."

Lila pulled out a chair after she filled a mug with coffee. Her insides churned like a handful of walnuts destined for the nut mill.

"I was part of an interesting exchange with Suzanne and her mother at the store."

Aunt Cathy's shoulder blades hit the back of her chair. Her mouth gaped open. "They were at Window Shopping?" she asked.

Lila widened her eyes and continued, "Mrs. Matthews suggested to Suzanne she should register for wedding gifts with the store when the time comes."

"Real...ly." Aunt Cathy strung out each syllable to emphasize her surprise.

"It's what followed Mrs. Matthews's suggestion that surprised me."

Cathy leaned in, pressing her full waist against the table's edge. "Explain."

"I don't think Suzanne cares one way or another if Conrad proposes. It's the way she responded to the suggestion and the ice in her eyes."

"She never was a good fit for our Conrad." Aunt Cathy resumed her ramrod position in the chair.

"That's not all that happened. I took their gift down to Albright Jewelers for engraving."

"Aha, aha."

"When I was back in my car, waiting for it to warm up, I spotted Conrad walking into the store."

If she was surprised, Aunt Cathy didn't show it. "And?" She shrugged as if she needed more to make a full assessment of the situation.

"What do you mean, 'and'? Isn't it obvious?"

Cathy scowled. "No, it isn't. Not to me."

Lila folded her arms across her chest. "He's decided to propose to Suzanne."

"That the conclusion you've jumped to all on your own?"

"He told me he wanted to get his life in order. Well, I guess this is it."

Cathy shook her head. "You can't assume anything for sure until you talk with him."

"He walked into a jewelry store and after our argument a few days ago, I'm not surprised. It all makes sense now."

Cathy placed her hands on full hips. "Well, your day was certainly full, wasn't it? Now I understand why you didn't sleep at all last night. What did you two have words about?"

Heat rose up Lila's neck. "He accused me of running off to the big city, and I reminded him of the responsibilities we both made to other people. It's the same old argument rearing its head."

"Don't you dare search for a reason to run. Not again. Remember when we talked about the applesauce skins in the sauce?"

Lila paused, giving merit to what her aunt was reminding her of—that unsettled issues tend to resurface in life.

"Honey, God's already forgiven you for the hurt you've caused Conrad. It's time you forgive yourself, and Conrad has to do the very exact thing. I swear. You two are your own worst enemies."

Lila drank from her mug, the caffeinated brew working its magic. "It's too late, Aunt Cathy. I won't interfere. Conrad's made up his mind. It's time for me to go home." The words left her mouth, but in her heart, she realized New York would never be the same special place on Earth it used to be.

"Are you going to tell him you're leaving?"

Lila refrained from answering for a minute fighting the urge to be sick. The coffee she'd enjoyed moments ago now working against her. "I think I'll save him the awkward truth of telling me he's proposed."

"Oh, Lila." Aunt Cathy got up from the table and opened her arms. "How I wish you'd change your mind. Something about all this doesn't sit well with me."

Lila stood from the table and walked into her aunt's open arms, the scent of lavender closing in all around her. She was going to miss these loving arms. "Thank you, for everything," she whispered. She'd remember this moment. The last hours before she left Conrad.

Aunt Cathy placed her hands on Lila's arms and looked her straight in the eyes. "This has been your home since your parents' terrible accident, and it always will be for as long as the good Lord gives me."

"You're too good to me." Lila gazed at her aunt as if for the last time cataloging every detail like a new item that arrived at the store. Although they spoke on the phone often, she wasn't sure when the next time they'd be together. Her new life was slipping away. "I guess I'd better get going. I want a head start to beat this snow."

"OK, but I still don't like this. Did you call the airport and make sure your flight is running on time, or even scheduled? Sometimes they cancel flights due to bad weather coming in."

"Already did that before I came down. There's no snow in New York. All I need to do is get to the airport. It'll be OK," Lila used a tone filled with confidence she wished was real.

"Fine, huh? I'm not sure about that. You never did like driving in snow."

"Don't forget I grew up here. I still remember how to drive in winter weather."

Aunt Cathy offered up her hands. "When's the last time you drove in a snowstorm? You told me you take cabs everywhere in New York."

Lila walked her mug over to the kitchen sink. "I'm going to miss all your mothering. No one in New York cares like you do."

"That's an easy solution. Don't go back." Aunt Cathy slapped her hands together as if the discussion was over.

Lila exhaled, "I must, and there's a part of you that realizes as much."

"Will you do me a favor? Call me when you reach the airport. Phone service is sporadic with an approaching storm. I'll be sick with worry until that phone rings."

Lila turned and kissed her aunt's cheek and headed for her room. "I will. Now you have a terrific day at the store today and sell, sell, sell those platters."

"Still as stubborn as you were as a child."

Lila smiled at her aunt's scolding, but her heart was anything but happy.

27

Conrad woke surprised he'd slept as well as he had. Then again, his life was finally in a place that made absolute sense to him—the future he desired within his grasp. The last time he spoke with Lila, he'd been a total jerk. What was he thinking? Losing his temper never solved anything. Why didn't he turn around and apologize? There were times when his short fuse got the best of him, causing walls to erect and regrets to move in. He'd stormed off like an immature kid, but he'd make it up to her today.

Everything was planned out on how he'd handle this. After a quick shower, he'd grab a thermos of coffee and head down to Window Shopping. After working there for almost a month, building the ski chalet, he remembered it was usually quiet first thing in the morning, but this was the day before Christmas Eve. He hoped it wasn't busy, but if it was, he'd wait for a reprieve. He needed time to say what he wanted to say to her. After rehearsing plenty last night as he lay in bed before falling asleep. He was ready.

He was about to step out the door when a series of phone calls left him dealing with an irate client who demanded to speak to him and settle an issue. The misunderstanding set him back a good two hours. Now, finally, he was on his way to the store, surprised to find the road conditions treacherous. He'd thought the storm wasn't expected until much later.

He parked a block away from the store. Lifting his

collar to shield his face from the snow, he stomped down the sidewalk, his footsteps sinking deep. His heart slammed against his chest—pure adrenaline. Finally, things were going to work out as they were meant to five years ago.

He opened the door to the store and walked in, oblivious to the Christmas music but not to the number of customers waiting to check out. He scanned the room for Lila. To his surprise, he found Melanie's mother, Mrs. Lange, behind the counter.

After she'd checked out three customers, Conrad inched his way to the counter. "Hello, Mrs. Lange. I'd like to speak to Lila."

Mrs. Lange restacked a pile of flyers. "I thought she left. That's why I'm here."

Conrad's throat seized. "What do you mean?" The words stuck on his tongue like sticky taffy in a little boy's teeth.

Mrs. Lange shrugged her shoulders. "She told Melanie she needed me to take over full-time starting today. Her Aunt Cathy is coming in this afternoon. She might be able to help you out."

Conrad rapped his knuckles three times on the counter. "Thanks, that helps." He turned and headed for the front door, battling his greatest fear—that he was too late. He ran back to his truck, fighting the wind and snow that pelted his face. His only concern was to find Lila.

He jumped in his truck, threw it into four-wheel-drive and fought the slow traffic over to Lila's. Once there, Conrad rang the doorbell at least half a dozen times. He wanted to be sure that Mrs. Williams heard it. The adrenaline surging earlier now began to fray into tiny shards inside of him.

The front door whooshed opened. Cathy stood in the doorway. "For goodness' sake, Conrad, what on earth has gotten into you?" She clutched at her sweater, drawing it up over her neck. "Come on in out of this storm."

He ambled in. Melting snow dripped off his boots falling onto the small foyer rug like a melting ice cream cone on a summer's day.

Cathy closed the interior door. "I can pretty well guess why you're here."

Conrad brushed the snow off of his head. It scattered into the air throughout the room. "I'm hoping Lila is…"

"She left thirty minutes ago, possibly forty-five. I'm not sure you can catch her. This storm came early. I'm worried about her. She's not used to driving in this kind of weather."

Conrad wrestled with the panic that slammed every emergency button in his head. He turned to leave, not wanting to waste another minute.

"Do you think calling her is a good idea?" Cathy suggested. Worry splashed across her face like freckles on a schoolgirl. She opened both doors for Conrad and stood facing the onslaught of snow and sleet.

Conrad stepped out onto the concrete stoop. He raised a gloved hand against the weather. "I don't want her distracted while driving. It could cause an accident. I'll take the back roads. Don't worry; I'll catch up to her."

Aunt Cathy nodded. "You're right. Be safe out there. The news is reporting another foot of snow until this system moves through the area."

Conrad gave Cathy a wave good-bye and hustled back to his truck. He tore down the road a little fast for the conditions, but this wasn't the first snowstorm he'd manhandled in five years, the way it was for Lila. "Keep her from harm, Lord," he prayed and hit the gas toward Highway 42.

28

Once on the highway, Lila refused to think about Conrad. As far as she was concerned, he left her the day he walked into Albright Jewelers. The thought steeled her nerves as she made her way down Highway 42, headed for the airport.

Although she departed early, hoping to beat the prediction of heavy snow, her tight grip on the steering wheel confirmed it was already too late. She forced tired eyes on the road, wishing she'd slept better. Visibility was awful, a few yards ahead of her vehicle. The road ahead loomed like a haunted castle waiting to devour her. Conrad was right when he said she'd always been a scaredy-cat over winter storms, and today was no exception. *No, no, no. I will not think of Conrad.* She lowered her speed and pressed on, but at this rate, she wouldn't make it to the airport until tomorrow. She could almost reach over and touch her fear, sitting right next to her in the passenger seat. The plows wouldn't be out yet—they'd wait for the storm to subside. "Don't panic," she said out loud. "Take it easy."

It was right after she'd passed Fish Creek, heading for Egg Harbor, when she spotted deer. By instinct, she lifted her foot off the gas and slammed on the brakes. *Oh, oh!* The tires locked. The truck slid on a thick layer of ice. Her eyes shot to the driver's-side mirror. The back end of the vehicle moved forward in an unnatural angle.

Lila shrieked. She repositioned her hands on the wheel and tightened her grip, causing her knuckles to appear like snow-topped mountain peaks. She squeezed her eyelids closed. She'd lost control. "Stay with me, Lord!" she cried.

She bounced forward in her seat avoiding the steering wheel by mere inches. The contents of her purse flew across the dashboard and onto the floor. An abrupt slam brought everything to a deathly silence. The motor idled. She peered through squinted eyes. Fear gripped her. Was the vehicle totaled? She'd never done that before. Panic rose in her throat. She was alone, on a highway less traveled during the winter months, in the middle of a snowstorm, without cellphone service. How long would it be until someone came along to help her? She turned to find the passenger side of the vehicle smashed into a snowbank right next to a utility pole. She exhaled, relieving the tension in her chest that disguised itself as the worst heartburn of her life.

Up ahead, a family of deer emerged from the protection of the forest. Lila watched the doe as she took calculated steps across the road. The others followed close behind her. They moved in sync, aware of each other's signals, until they reached safety on the other side, soon disappearing into the forest. They were a family—their natural instincts guiding them away from danger yet drawing them near to protect what was most important—each other.

Lila lowered her head and pressed her lips against her hands on the wheel. She couldn't remember when she'd witnessed anything as natural or as beautiful. She began to question every move she made over the last two days and realized she repeated the same mistake. The one she regretted over and over again—leaving Conrad.

She picked up the contents of her purse and reached for the gift Uncle Elmer gave her. She brought it close to her heart and hoped the gift inside wasn't damaged. Uncle Elmer predicted the time to open it would reveal itself to her, and it was right in front of her.

Lila tore at the wrapping paper and lifted the cover off the box. Peeling back the tissue paper, she revealed a miniature snow globe protected by a layer of bubble wrap. She sighed with relief. Nothing broken. With gentle nudging, she lifted it up, the box falling away to the side. Sparkly snow dust glittered inside and rested on the cedar shake roof of a small Cape Cod. The tiniest white picket fence protected the yard. It reminded her of the home she and Conrad talked about sharing one day, and Uncle Elmer's advice not to forget the very first dreams of her life. Conrad had always talked about building the house for their family.

The truth hit her so profoundly Lila sat motionless for a moment. She swallowed hard. Her throat as dry as one of her first attempts baking scones. Her fingers tightened around the globe. Aunt Cathy was right. God forgave her a long time ago. Now she must forgive herself and Conrad should do the same. Once they accomplished that, their lives would be whole again.

Thump, thump, thump! Lila's heart pounded in her ears. She placed the globe on the passenger seat next to her. If she could manage to get the vehicle out of the snow bank, she'd make her way back to Sister Bay. She must find Conrad before he proposed. She picked up her phone and tried Cathy. No service. *Rats.*

She flipped on the hazard signals, zipped up her parka, and slipped on her hat and gloves. When she opened her door, a wall of snow hit her square in the face. Her eyes stung from the mix of sleet and snow. She wasn't about to let weather deter her now. Determination and grit melded inside of her and propelled her feet forward. She'd figure out a way to get herself out of here and back to Sister Bay. She only hoped it wasn't too late.

29

Lila knelt in the snow to check underneath the car. She placed her palms on the frozen ground and surveyed the damage. In all honesty, she wasn't sure what looked good and what didn't. Everything appeared OK except for the right front tire. It was buried in the snow. *Oh, no.* That wasn't good. She remembered the advice her father had given her years ago. 'When stuck in the snow, rock yourself out'. There was only one way to find out if his advice would work. She stomped through the snow back to the front of the vehicle and slid behind the wheel. She shifted into drive but hesitated. That utility pole was too close.

She exhaled a frustrated sigh. She'd have to inch in reverse first. Wasn't that how it was done? She couldn't remember, so she slid the gear into reverse and moved her foot from the brake to the accelerator and gave it a jolt of gas. The tires grabbed hold bolting the vehicle backward. She screamed and slammed on the brakes and slipped the gear into park.

She opened the door and stepped out into the storm again. She wrapped her arms around herself and viewed the results. The SUV was wedged deeper into the snowbank. Great. There was no getting out of this. She'd need someone to pull her out. Now what? She could walk until she found service for her phone. But she'd seen enough horror movies to remember that wasn't smart. You were supposed to stay with the vehicle, not venture out alone in a snowstorm. She leaned against the bumper. *How am I going to get out of here?*

A gust of wind caught hold of the snow and whipped it across her face. Her feet were like bricks as she trudged back to the vehicle and climbed inside. She shucked off her gloves, shivered, and rubbed her palms together to bring some warmth to them. Her eyes scanned the interior, hoping to find an answer. She caught sight of the snow globe and lifted it to her heart. She rubbed her thumb across the glass as if it held magical powers that could whisk her away and return her to Sister Bay like Dorothy in The Wizard of Oz. Tears slid down her cheeks. She laid her head onto the headrest. "I tried to come back to you, Conrad. Forgive me."

A light coming from the road caught in her peripheral vision. Her heart jumped ten feet. She wiped away her tears. Yes! Yes! She couldn't believe God's provision. She got out of the car, forgetting to close the door behind her, and waved her arms. "Stop, please?" Was the truck slowing? It was so hard to tell. As difficult as it was, she forced her feet from the ground and continued jumping while shouting, "Help, help!" She was certain she must appear like a half-crazed woman in peril, but she was desperate to get back to Sister Bay.

Shielding her eyes from the sleet that hit her face, she blinked hard. There was no way she'd let the driver pass her by. She'd run straight out into the road. Visibility was near impossible. Wait a minute. The approaching vehicle was a red truck.

Conrad drove a red truck.

The driver made a sharp turn onto the side of the road and parked. The door opened, and a large man stepped out and strode straight toward her as if he was in total command of the situation and the weather was an insignificant factor.

Conrad! How was this possible? Lila wasn't sure whether to laugh or to cry. He found her.

Without saying a word, he opened up his arms for her like a mother bear.

"Conrad." She couldn't run fast enough. Fighting the snow, she almost tripped over her own feet. Her arms clamped around him. There she was as safe as if she were sitting in Aunt Cathy's kitchen drinking a cup of coffee.

"Oh, Lila, Lila," he breathed. "I've been tracking you down all morning." He kissed her face over and over. "Are you all right? I didn't want to call for fear you'd end up in a ditch and that's exactly where I found you. You're not hurt, are you?"

Why would he be searching for her? She tilted her head to peer up at him. "I'm OK, but why were you out in the storm?"

He took a step back, releasing his hold on her but kept her hands gripped firmly in his. "I'd be a fool to let the love of my life slip through my fingers again. It was all my fault for not going after you the first time."

Lila placed her hands on his face. "No, it wasn't your fault. It was mine. I should have come home and back to you. I was a fool."

"I think it's time we forgive ourselves and each other for what we did or didn't do."

He raised her chin with his finger. Their eyes locked. "I always thought you'd come back to me, Lila."

Lila swallowed back the tears that wanted to burst from the five-year dam she kept them behind. "And I thought you'd come after me."

"Does this mean we forgive each other?" he asked.

"I guess that's up to us."

Conrad flashed her his infectious smile. "It's time."

"It would be so wonderful to let it go," Lila said.

"I forgive you, Lila." In Conrad eyes she recognized the same pain she'd been carrying all these years.

"And I forgive you. But there's one more important part to this. We need to forgive ourselves, too, so we can move forward."

"You're right."

Lila fought back tears. "How could we be so blind?"

Conrad gave a tilt of his head. "I think we needed to learn a lesson."

Lila widened her eyes like a surprised doe. "Conrad, where do we go from here? What about Suzanne?"

Conrad shook his head. "It hasn't been right between Suzanne and me for so long. Part of our relationship worked, but most of it didn't. In the end, we both came to terms with that."

Lila covered her mouth with her hand. "I could sense something was wrong the other day when she and her mother stopped in Window Shopping."

Conrad rested his gaze on her with a softness that melted her heart. "For so many years, I tried denying my love for you, but I was never successful."

Lila wiped the tears from the corners of her eyes. "Oh, Conrad, I've waited so long for those words. You're my one and only love. It's the reason all my past relationships failed because I was still in love with you."

He nodded. "We were still in love with each other. Our dreams are still waiting for us. I think it's time we made them a reality."

Lila shrugged. "What am I going to do? I need to get to New York."

Conrad's smile transformed into the grin she loved. She'd never have to miss it again.

"I'm not sure I understand computers, but I got an earful the other day today from my sister Cassie. Correct me if I'm wrong, but can't you write sitting on a pier with your feet in the water on a laptop as easy as you could behind a desk in Manhattan?"

Lila let a slight giggle escape her. Conrad's perceptions on her work were adorable. "You're right about that part, but I still need to get to New York at some point and straighten things out with Andrea. I may even need a new editor."

"What do you say we'll figure those things out together?" He retrieved something small from his oversized pocket. Despite the wind and the relentless snow, Conrad bent and knelt down on one knee. To Lila's surprise, he revealed a blue velvet box in the palm of his hand. When he opened it, an emerald cut diamond ring caught a fleeting ray of sun before it disappeared behind a snow cloud. It sparkled with an undeniable brilliance like a bride on her father's arm.

"Ooh." Lila brought her fingers to her lips. Her eyes filled with tears of absolute joy. It was breathtaking and spectacular and this moment in time took her by complete and utter surprise. A nervous laugh escaped her.

"Lila Clark, you are the love of my life. I will love you forever, until my last breath. Will you marry me and make all of my dreams come true?"

Lila exhaled. For a moment, time stopped. The man she'd loved forever asked her to marry him. Now she understood what her aunt and Melanie told her so many times—that she needed to put the past behind her and give her heart some breathing room. She'd followed the footsteps of God's design for her life without even realizing it, and His plan was giving her hope and a brand-new future. *Thank you, Lord, for leading me home.* "Yes," she breathed. "Yes, yes, Conrad, you've always been my only love. Absolutely nothing would make me happier. I will marry you."

Conrad rose and slid the ring on her finger. A perfect fit exactly like they were. He placed a gentle hand behind the nape of her neck and drew her toward him. He kissed her with all the passion of a man in love. Not that of a boyfriend of years ago, or a rekindled love of recent months together, but that of a man who found his soulmate.

Lila inched closer as if he were a warming sun after a rain. She pressed into him, and the raging storm around them faded away. His lips on hers made sense of the world. She'd found him again—her prince. For the first time ever, she understood the scripture she was taught so many times: "…and the two shall become one."

"Let's go home," he whispered in her ear, "or we'll be late for choir practice."

A smile spread across Lila's face. "Sounds like heaven to me."

30

Mr. Abbott lifted his baton and hit the edge of the music stand. Tap, tap, tap. The choir came to life like a wound-up toy under a Christmas tree. Lila straightened her shoulders. She peeked toward the tenor section of the choir. Conrad winked at her as if he expected her gaze. They shared a secret. Lila twisted the engagement ring around her finger and returned his smile. The ring, heavy with its oversized diamond, reminded Lila of her journey back to Conrad, her one true love.

In unison and on cue, the sopranos sang the first lines of "Silent Night" a cappella. A hush, like clouds gathering on a summer day, spread across the congregation. Lila fought the urge to cry. Her aunt was sitting next to Conrad's parents. In the years ahead, she'd always find comfort in her soft arms or strong advice. Melanie, Jack, and the twins took refuge in the back row, uncertain if one of the newest members of their family would decide to join the choir, invited or not.

Lila's call to Andrea earlier that day hadn't been easy, but once Lila told her the news of the engagement everything changed. Lila reminded her of the wager they entered, and Andrea laughed through her tears. For the first time since everything changed, Lila wished she could be in two places at one time.

When the service was over, Pastor Phelps invited the congregation downstairs for fellowship, tempting the audience with Christmas cookies, kringle pastries, and coffee. Conrad towered over most of the crowd. He found Lila in an instant. This was how life already changed. A shift in how they both moved through the world—no longer as individuals but as a pair according to God's great design. They were blessed in finding one another again. Lila couldn't stop thanking God for the best Christmas present she'd ever received.

"Let's catch them while they're still together. My mother will draw fifty people around her in less than five minutes if we let her." Conrad whispered in Lila's ear and urged her toward a linen-clad table in the center of the room where both families were seated.

Lila tossed her head back in a pleasant laugh. She'd been laughing a lot since Conrad's proposal. The day when her life turned in a direction she never dreamed possible. "Aunt Cathy's the same way. I must say, they are well-connected with the parish."

He placed a gentle hand on the small of her back and guided her through the crowd. Lila watched Conrad mouth, "Follow us," as they passed Uncle Elmer and a short while later to Jack, who was doing his best to maneuver a double stroller.

"It's awfully nice to lay eyes on you both again, Lila." Mrs. Hamilton sipped from her cup of coffee. She winked at Aunt Cathy, and this time, Lila didn't miss it.

Lila slipped her right hand over her left to conceal the ring. She refused to offer an explanation to Aunt Cathy when Conrad dropped her off at home yesterday. It was as if she and her aunt were on opposite sides of a debate team, but Lila managed to delay the answers to her questions and explained it would all be clear after the Christmas concert. The time to make good on that promise arrived.

"Personally, I've waited long enough. I'd like to understand what's going on," Aunt Cathy appealed. She pushed aside her plate as if in protest, refusing to eat the almond kringle and Christmas cookies until she was satisfied.

Lila shot Conrad a sideward glance followed by a snicker—dragging this out was becoming quite fun. Lila was reminded of how much she enjoyed stringing along her readers with tension throughout her books. Funny, that was the first time she'd thought about writing.

Jack and Melanie sidled up to the table. After seating his wife, Jack pushed the stroller forward and backward in a smooth, well-practiced move that kept the babies satisfied. Melanie beamed at her husband's newfound talent and nodded at Lila as if to confirm the transition.

"Yes, we're all present. What are you two hiding?" Melanie asked, giving credence to Cathy's protest who followed Melanie's question with a *hmpf*.

Conrad cleared his throat.

Lila wasn't certain, but Conrad appeared nervous, almost fidgety. She rested her hand on his back and gave him a reassuring nod.

"Something out of this world wonderful happened yesterday." He peered at Lila and drew her toward him. "The love of my life has agreed to marry me."

Conrad raised Lila's left hand, brought it to his lips, and kissed it.

Aunt Cathy gasped. "So, that's the big secret?"

Mrs. Hamilton started clapping. "Glory be to heaven above."

The two women grabbed each other's hands in the

excitement. "We'll be related." Aunt Cathy gushed.

"Congratulations, son." Conrad's father stood from the table and reached across to shake Conrad's hand.

Melanie was the first to grab Lila into a hug. "Come here, you." She gave Lila an extra squeeze. "Let's see if Conrad did a good job with that rock."

Lila welcomed her embrace and offered her hand to Melanie realizing they made it back to each other. Friends again, and this time, for life.

Melanie held Lila's engaged hand in her own. "It's beautiful like you and Conrad are together. I've been praying for this all along. It was so obvious to everyone that you two fell in love again. I'm so happy for you both."

"Happy enough to be my matron-of-honor?" Lila brought her hands together as if in prayer.

Melanie laid a hand on her chest. "Absolutely. Oh, Lila, I'd be honored."

"You and Aunt Cathy told me since I arrived that I was exactly where God wanted me. You were both right. It's amazing."

Melanie rolled her eyes. "And you actually listened. I thought you were leaving and going back to New York."

"I did leave, but in my most desperate moment, God opened my eyes to His plan for me."

Melanie's mouth gaped open. "OK, you need to fill me in on what happened out there."

A grin of a school girl spread across Lila's face. She was so ecstatically happy. Her life completely changed course in a matter of hours. "How's coffee on Monday at the store? I was toying with an idea for an after-Christmas sale and could use your insight. Mornings are usually quiet."

Melanie smiled and wiggled a finger back and forth. "Do you realize we've gone through a role reversal here?"

"How does that shoe fit?" Lila asked.

Before Melanie could answer Cathy interrupted. "I'm next," she stood in line as if waiting for her number to be called at the meat counter.

"She's all yours. We'll talk later," Melanie whispered and walked toward Jack, who was in conversation with Conrad and his father.

Aunt Cathy searched Lila's eyes and then pulled her into a warm embrace. "Your love story reminds me of one of my favorite scriptures—'For I know the plans I have for you…' I believe you know the rest."

"Know it? I've lived it…'declares the LORD, plans for welfare and not for evil, to give you a future and a hope.' I'll never forget to trust in His plan for my life again for as long as I live."

"Congratulations, sweetheart." She tipped her head and lowered her voice. "This is what Mabel and I were praying would happen from the day you walked back into the village."

Lila rolled her head from side to side as if scolding a small child. "I noticed the winks and nods between you but didn't figure it out until today."

Aunt Cathy bent her head and gazed upward. "We didn't do it alone. By the way, what are you going to do about the meeting in New York?"

"Funny you should ask," Lila crossed her arms over her chest. "I received a text message from Andrea last night. The meeting was postponed until after the holidays due to the impending winter storm heading their way."

Aunt Cathy laughed. "The same storm you were driving in to get to the meeting."

Lila nodded. "Yep."

"Wow." Cathy placed her hands on the side of her head. "If that's not a message from above, I'm not sure what is."

"Conrad and I are flying out together after the holiday. I'm planning on pitching my new book series to Jim and the new publishing house. I'm hoping he's open to the children's mystery series. If not, Andrea and I have a new hurdle to overcome finding a brand-new editor and publishing house for me. Everything will work out as it should."

Cathy brought her hands together. "That's my girl. I'm proud of you, Lila. You've finally come home to us, and Conrad, well that young man has been like a son to me for years. Soon, it'll be legitimate."

Lila pulled her aunt into her arms and hugged her with a brand-new fierceness for life. A Christmas miracle happened. She was as blessed as Melanie was with her newborn twins.

"So, when's the wedding?" Mr. Hamilton's voice boomed above the small group.

"As soon as possible," Conrad and Lila responded at almost the same time. They beamed smiles to the group in the bliss they created for their families and each other.

Aunt Cathy turned to address the other parishioners in the room. "We're having a wedding. How's that for the best Christmas present ever?" Hoots and hollers and applause followed her announcement.

"If you need a minister, I'm available New Year's Eve," Pastor Phelps said with a wide grin. He raised his coffee cup as if to offer a toast.

Conrad stretched out a hand and encouraged Lila into his arms. He gave her the familiar gaze—the one that told her what was coming.

"Here in church?" she asked, now wearing one of his devilish grins.

He nodded. "I'm afraid so," and bent his head and kissed her.

ACKNOWLEDGEMENTS

Special thanks to my critique group members for your astute listening skills and your critical eyes, for all of your encouragement, and your boundless support that propels me forward in this glorious journey. An enormous thank you to all my editors, you know who you are. Finally, to my parents who provided me with a childhood that allowed my imagination to flourish and a faith that grounds my walk in this life I am blessed to live.

BIOGRAPHY

Christine Schimpf was born and raised in a small town in southeastern Wisconsin. Growing up she enjoyed fishing with her dad, bicycle riding, and climbing trees. She attended a Catholic elementary school where she met her husband in second grade.

She earned a Bachelor of Arts degree in public relations and English writing at the University of Wisconsin-Whitewater. During college, she entered a national essay competition and won a seat at the Women's as Leaders conference in Washington D.C. She's a member of the American Christian Fiction Writers Association and the Romance Writers of America and the United States Tennis Association.

When she's not writing, she enjoys planting seeds and flowers in the spring, golfing and kayaking in the summer, and playing indoor tennis over the winter months. She and her dog Rudy walk every day unless the temperature drops below 20 degrees. Presently, she lives on five acres in the country with her husband and golden retriever.

Christine loves to hear from her readers. Please visit her website at christineschimpf.webs.com for author updates, blog posts, and more information on all of her books. Her email is cschimpf57@yahoo.com.

Thank you

We appreciate you reading this Prism title. For other Christian fiction and clean-and-wholesome stories, please visit our on-line bookstore at
www.prismbookgroup.com.

For questions or more information, contact us at
customer@pelicanbookgroup.com.

Prism is an imprint of
Pelican Book Group
www.PelicanBookGroup.com

Connect with Us
www.facebook.com/Pelicanbookgroup
www.twitter.com/pelicanbookgrp

To receive news and specials, subscribe to our bulletin
http://pelink.us/bulletin

May God's glory shine through
this inspirational work of fiction.

AMDG

You Can Help!

At Pelican Book Group it is our mission to entertain readers with fiction that uplifts the Gospel. It is our privilege to spend time with you awhile as you read our stories.

We believe you can help us to bring Christ into the lives of people across the globe. And you don't have to open your wallet or even leave your house!

Here are 3 simple things you can do to help us bring illuminating fiction™ to people everywhere.

1) If you enjoyed this book, write a positive review. Post it at online retailers and websites where readers gather. And share your review with us at reviews@pelicanbookgroup.com (this does give us permission to reprint your review in whole or in part.)

2) If you enjoyed this book, recommend it to a friend in person, at a book club or on social media.

3) If you have suggestions on how we can improve or expand our selection, let us know. We value your opinion. Use the contact form on our web site or e-mail us at customer@pelicanbookgroup.com

God Can Help!

Are you in need? The Almighty can do great things for you. Holy is His Name! He has mercy in every generation. He can lift up the lowly and accomplish all things. Reach out today.

Do not fear: I am with you; do not be anxious: I am your God. I will strengthen you, I will help you, I will uphold you with my victorious right hand.
~Isaiah 41:10 (NAB)

We pray daily, and we especially pray for everyone connected to Pelican Book Group—that includes you! If you have a specific need, we welcome the opportunity to pray for you. Share your needs or praise reports at http://pelink.us/pray4us

Free Book Offer

We're looking for booklovers like you to partner with us! Join our team of influencers today and periodically receive free eBooks and exclusive offers.

For more information
Visit http://pelicanbookgroup.com/booklovers